Books by Ed Dunlop

The Terrestria Chronicles
The Sword, the Ring, and the Parchment
The Quest for Seven Castles
The Search for Everyman
The Crown of Kuros
The Dragon's Egg
The Golden Lamps
The Great War

Tales from Terrestria
The Quest for Thunder Mountain
The Golden Dagger

Jed Cartwright Adventure Series
The Midnight Escape
The Lost Gold Mine
The Comanche Raiders
The Lighthouse Mystery
The Desperate Slave
The Midnight Rustlers

The Young Refugees Series
Escape to Liechtenstein
The Search for the Silver Eagle
The Incredible Rescues

Sherlock Jones Detective Series
Sherlock Jones and the Assassination Plot
Sherlock Jones and the Willoughby Bank Robbery
Sherlock Jones and the Missing Diamond
Sherlock Jones and the Phantom Airplane
Sherlock Jones and the Hidden Coins
Sherlock Jones and the Odyssey Mystery

The 1,000-Mile Journey

The Quest for Seven Castles

THE TERRESTRIA CHRONICLES: BOOK TWO

An allegory
by Ed Dunlop

cross & crown
PUBLISHING
RINGGOLD, GEORGIA

www.TalesOfCastles.com
Cover Art by Laura Lea Sencabaugh and Wayne Coley

The quest for seven castles : an allegory / by Ed Dunlop.
Dunlop, Ed.
[Ringgold, Ga.] : Cross and Crown Publishing, c2006
209 p. ; 22 cm.
Terrestria chronicles Bk. 2
Dewey Call # 813.54
ISBN 0978552318
ISBN 978-0-9785523-1-2

"When King Emmanuel sends Prince Josiah
on a difficult journey to various castles across the kingdom,
the young prince is unprepared for the dangers he will face." –Cover

Dunlop, Ed.
Middle ages juvenile fiction.
Christian life juvenile fiction.
Allegories.
Fantasy

Second Edition
Printed and bound in the United States of America

That you and I might grow
to be like our King

And beside this, giving all diligence,
add to your faith VIRTUE;
and to virtue KNOWLEDGE;
and to knowledge TEMPERANCE;
and to temperance PATIENCE;
and to patience GODLINESS;
and to godliness BROTHERLY KINDNESS;
and to brotherly kindness CHARITY.
For if these things be in you and abound,
they make you that ye shall neither
be barren nor unfruitful
in the knowledge of our Lord Jesus Christ.

– II Peter 1:5-8

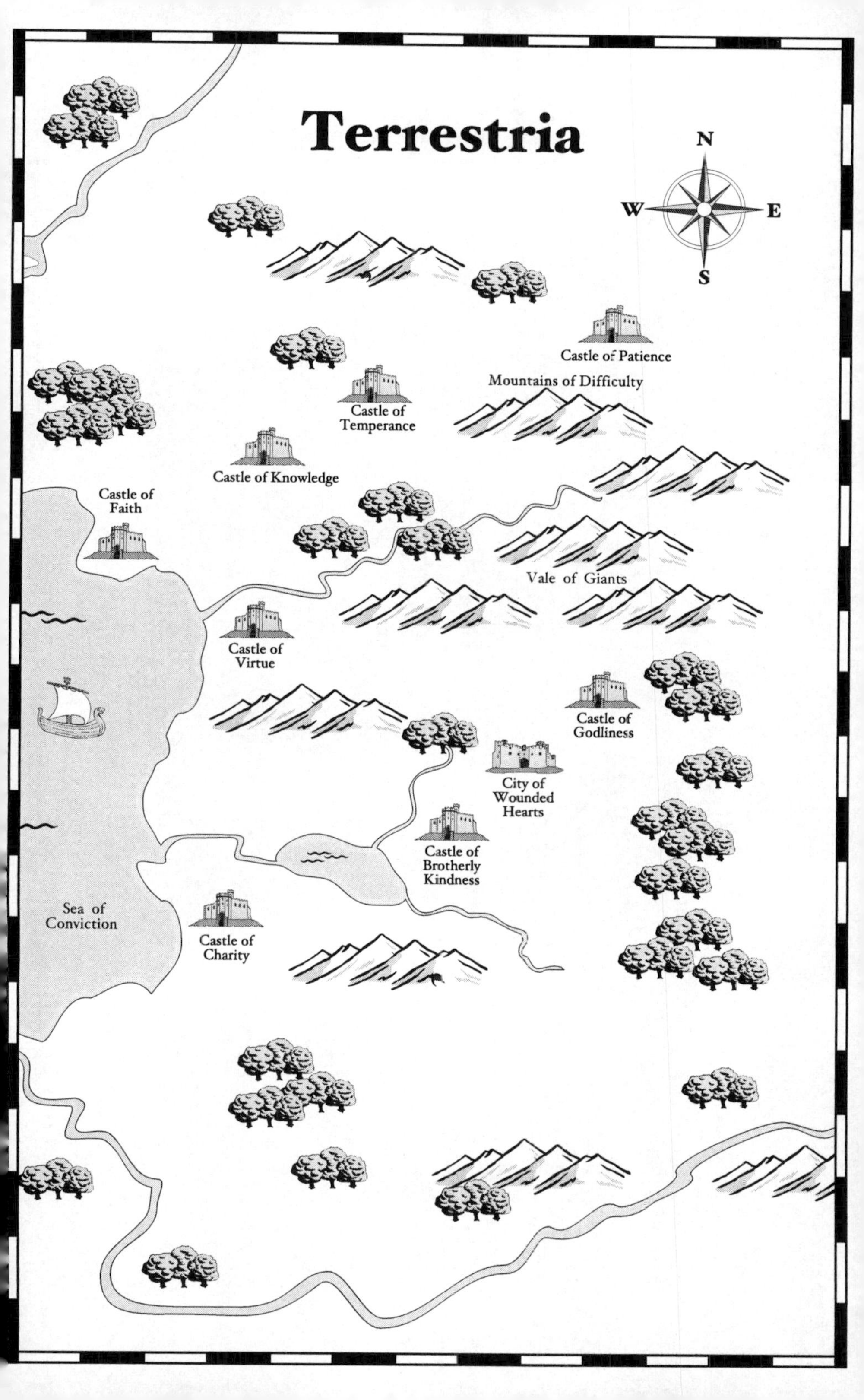
Terrestria
N
W
E
S
Castle of Patience
Mountains of Difficulty
Castle of Temperance
Castle of Knowledge
Castle of Faith
Vale of Giants
Castle of Virtue
Castle of Godliness
City of Wounded Hearts
Castle of Brotherly Kindness
Sea of Conviction
Castle of Charity

Chapter One

In a land far away and a time long ago, the early morning sun glistened on polished armor as a mounted knight rode swiftly along the King's highway. The breath of the knight's powerful white horse hung in the cool morning air as he thundered past awakening farms and sleepy villages. The knight was riding hard. The clatter of the animal's hooves rang like a blacksmith's hammer across the stillness of the moors.

In the distance, the same rising sun glistened on the white marble walls of a majestic castle, painting them with pastel hues of orange, pink and violet. The castle, situated high atop a rocky palisade, overlooked a quiet region in the peaceful kingdom of Terrestria. King Emmanuel, Lord of all Terrestria, had constructed the castle of the finest materials. Situated between the Sea of Conviction and the Village of Dedication, the castle had high, sturdy walls, even taller towers, massive gates and a deep, wide moat. Two garrisons of knights under Captain Assurance and Captain Diligence walked the battlements night and day, guarding the walls of the Castle of Faith, always on the lookout for danger.

The stalwart knight leaned forward in the saddle, urging his powerful horse to even greater speed. The man's visor was down, concealing his face, but his glistening figure seemed to radiate a sense of urgency. He rode as though the slightest delay would mean failure for his mission.

High on the battlements of the Castle of Faith, an elderly man dressed in a splendid green doublet and shimmering white cloak stood talking with a slender young man. The youth wore a sleeveless jerkin of soft, pale deerskin, and a magnificent cloak of blue and gold.

"Sir Faithful," the youth said, leaning over the battlements of the castle and looking at the ground far below, "do you realize that I have now been at the Castle of Faith for an entire year? It was one year ago today that King Emmanuel came in the Coach of Grace and rescued me from the evil blacksmith, Argamor. What a year this has been!"

The old man smiled and stroked his long, white beard with the fingertips of both hands. "Has it already been a year, Prince Josiah? My, how time flies! Sometimes it seems that it was only yesterday that you came to the Castle of Faith." He chuckled gently as he turned and gazed lovingly at the young prince. "My, how one year at the castle has changed you! It was a skinny little wretch of a boy that entered the castle a year ago; but now I see before me a tall, handsome young prince."

Prince Josiah smiled, but there was not a trace of pride in his lively brown eyes. His heart thrilled with gratitude as he thought about the day that he had met the loving and gracious King. "I'll never forget what His Majesty did for me that day," he said softly. "Argamor and his evil henchmen were preparing to flog me, but King Emmanuel rescued me and brought me to the Castle of Faith!"

Just then the clatter of hooves arrested the attention of the elderly steward and the young prince, and they both looked down to see the knight on the white horse come thundering up to the castle gate. The rider drew back on the reins and brought his steed to a halt at the edge of the drawbridge, and the magnificent animal pranced and pawed the earth restlessly. The knight stood in the stirrups and raised his visor. "Halloo the Castle of Faith!"

"A messenger from His Majesty," Sir Faithful said quietly.

Prince Josiah stared at him in surprise. "From King Emmanuel? Sire, how can you tell?"

The old man smiled mysteriously. "Just wait. You shall soon learn that I am correct."

"Who approaches the castle?" The challenge came from the battlements of the gatehouse towering over the drawbridge.

"I am Sir Reliable," the knight answered in a deep voice that echoed off the castle walls. "I come from the Golden City with a message from His Majesty, King Emmanuel."

Josiah looked at Sir Faithful in astonishment. "Sire, you were right! Do you think that His Majesty is coming to the Castle of Faith today?"

Sir Faithful shook his head. "King Emmanuel could come today, and we must always be watching for his return, but this message is in regards to another matter."

"Enter, noble knight, and be recognized," the gatekeeper called, and as Prince Josiah and Sir Faithful watched from atop the wall, the knight rode forward and entered the castle.

Sir Faithful looked fondly at Josiah. "Remember the day that you came to the Castle of Faith? I still recall how surprised you were to learn that you had become a prince."

Josiah smiled. "I'm still amazed to think that King Emmanuel would adopt me," he confessed. He let out his breath in a long sigh of contentment. "Just think, Sir Faithful, I went from being a slave to being a prince in just one day! That's enough to overwhelm anyone!"

The old man chuckled. "I know."

"The very best part, sire, is that my chain of iniquity and my weight of guilt are gone forever. I have been set free! And I never have to return to the Dungeon of Condemnation! I love my King."

The young prince paused for a moment, reflecting on the goodness and grace of King Emmanuel. His heart was filled with gratitude. "I thank you, my King," he whispered softly.

Josiah's thoughts returned to the memorable day that King Emmanuel had ransomed him. He shuddered as he remembered the cruelty of Argamor and his evil henchmen, Evilheart and Lawofsin. For just a moment, he was back in the filthy coal yard of Argamor's blacksmith shop, and he could almost feel the ropes around his wrists as Lawofsin bound him to a yew tree in preparation for a flogging. He could still recall the terror he had felt as he waited for the stinging lash of the whip across his bare back. But the Coach of Grace had appeared just at that moment, and the cruel flogging had never taken place. King Emmanuel had stepped from the coach, rescued Josiah, and set him free from Argamor's tyranny. Josiah wept with the memory of that blessed day when the King of glory had adopted him and brought him to live as a prince in the Castle of Faith.

A page dressed in royal blue ascended the castle stairs just then and hurried across the sentry walk toward the old man and the boy. "A message from King Emmanuel, sire," the page said, bowing low and handing a parchment to Sir Faithful. "It has just arrived. It's for Prince Josiah."

"I thank you, William," the steward replied, taking the parchment from the boy. The page bowed again and hurried away. Sir Faithful unrolled the document and scanned the message.

"What does it say, sire?" Josiah begged, but Sir Faithful continued to read in silence. Josiah waited anxiously.

At last, the old man lowered the parchment and gazed at Josiah. "The message is for you, from His Majesty, King Emmanuel," he said slowly.

"I know, I know," Josiah said impatiently, without meaning to be impolite. "But what does it say? Why did King Emmanuel send a messenger all the way from the Golden City just for me? What does my King want?"

Sir Faithful turned and regarded him thoughtfully for a long moment before answering. "His Majesty wants you to leave the Castle of Faith."

"Leave the Castle of Faith?" A surge of panic arose within Josiah's breast, overwhelming him and choking off his breath. He struggled to speak. "But why? Where would I go?"

"King Emmanuel has ordered you to depart the Castle of Faith," the steward repeated. "You are to leave immediately."

Chapter Two

A cold sensation of fear flooded over the young prince as he heard Sir Faithful's words. "But why am I to leave, sire?" he asked in dismay. "The Castle of Faith is my home! I have no other! Where would I go?"

"These orders are from King Emmanuel," the steward said quietly but firmly, tapping the parchment with a wrinkled finger, "and they must be obeyed, my prince."

"But why, Sir Faithful? Why must I leave?" Prince Josiah was in anguish.

"You must obey your King's orders."

"But w-what have I d-done?" Josiah stammered. "Does this mean that I am no longer a prince? Is Emmanuel no longer my King? May I not continue to serve Him?" His eyes filled with tears. "His Majesty has promised never to cast me out, sire! I read that in the book! 'Him that cometh to me I will in no wise cast out.' It's in the book, sire, and it's a promise from King Emmanuel!"

The old man suddenly realized what Josiah was thinking. He laughed gently. "Josiah, Josiah. Your King is not casting you out; he is merely sending you on a journey."

"A journey, sire? A journey to what destination?"

"His Majesty wants you to undertake a quest to seven other castles within the kingdom of Terrestria," Sir Faithful replied, holding up the King's parchment and studying it. "The steward of each castle will give you a rare jewel, which is to be displayed on your Shield of Faith to show that you have completed that portion of the journey and attained that level of maturity. This is to be a journey of learning. You are to leave the Castle of Faith today and travel to the Castle of Virtue."

"The Castle of Virtue? Where is that, sire? How will I find it?"

"Your book will guide you."

"I have learned what faith is, but what is virtue?"

The old man paused. "Virtue is... virtue is manly courage, the courage and ability to choose what is right. One might also use the words *integrity*, *honor*, and *character*. A man of virtue is a man who can be trusted to do what is right."

"But why must I go to the Castle of Virtue?" Josiah questioned. "Why can I not stay here at the Castle of Faith?"

"This quest is to be a learning experience designed to develop certain character qualities within you," Sir Faithful replied. "King Emmanuel has planned for you to take this quest that you might learn and grow and become like him. I must warn you—the journey will not be easy. There will be obstacles and difficulties and dangers along the way, and you must overcome them in your quest for the castles. When you reach the seventh castle, you will find that you have been trained for service to your King."

"What are the names of the other castles?" Josiah asked, with a growing sense of uneasiness. He was beginning to realize the significance of the assignment, and he knew instinctively that the journey would be even more difficult than what the steward was describing. He was determined not to fail his King.

Sir Faithful glanced at the parchment. "After you have reached the Castle of Virtue, you must journey to the Castle of Knowledge. Then you must travel to the Castle of Temperance, the Castle of Patience, the Castle of Godliness and the Castle of Brotherly Kindness. Your final destination, the seventh castle, is the Castle of Charity. When you have reached that castle, your journey will be complete, and you will be ready for His Majesty's service."

"But sire, I am ready now," Josiah protested. "I love His Majesty and I will serve him forever."

"You have already served your King well," the old steward assured him, "but life as a servant of King Emmanuel is a continual journey of learning and growth. This quest that you are undertaking today is but a step in that longer journey."

The young prince suddenly felt very small and inadequate. "But I cannot do this alone! What if I fail my King?"

Sir Faithful smiled. "I am very glad to hear you say that, my prince. Your words are a good indication that you are indeed ready to undertake a journey such as this. If you were confident and unafraid at a time like this, I would fear that you were trusting in yourself, and that would surely lead to failure. In the ancient languages your very name, Josiah, means 'Emmanuel reigns', and you must never forget that your strength comes from a heart yielded to King Emmanuel."

"But how will I know which way to go, sire? What if I lose my way? What if Argamor or his men should stop me? Sir Faithful, can you not go with me? I don't want to go alone."

The old man held up one hand to silence Josiah's words. "I cannot accompany you, Prince Josiah, but you will not go alone. You have your book, and the dove will guide you." Just then, the snowy white dove that Josiah had seen about the castle swooped down and landed atop one of the merlons of the castle wall. The beautiful bird sat silently on the stonework, gazing at Josiah with dark, unblinking eyes.

"How will he guide me?" Josiah asked, studying the bird. "Can he speak?"

"He speaks in a still, small voice," Sir Faithful answered. "He knows the mind of King Emmanuel perfectly, and his guidance will always be in perfect harmony with the King's words found in your book. But you must always be diligent to listen for his voice, for his promptings are always gentle and are easily ignored. He will be with you throughout the entire journey, but it will be very easy for you to forget that he is there. Remember that his purpose in accompanying you is to cause you to know the will of your King and enable you to do it, but he will never be forceful or insistent. He will always leave the choices to you, but you would be wise to heed his counsel."

Josiah's eyes widened in sudden realization and he stepped closer to Sir Faithful. "Sire, I have heard his voice," he said eagerly, "when I was on top of the mountain in the Forest of Decision! It was his voice that told me to use the book to find my way!"

Sir Faithful nodded. "Aye, my prince. Learn to listen for his voice, for he will never lead you wrong. Obedience to his voice will guarantee success in your quest for the seven castles." He paused and looked at Josiah with eyes filled with compassion. "Always remember that you can send a petition to His Majesty at any time, day or night. Your King desires success for you in this quest, and he stands ready to answer your every petition."

Months earlier, the old steward had taught the young prince an incredible form of communication with his gentle sovereign—whenever Josiah desired to send a message to the King, all he had to do was write it out on a parchment, roll it up, and release it. Miraculous as it seemed, in an instant the petition would be delivered to His Majesty's throne room at the Golden City. Josiah had learned from experience that Emmanuel was eager to receive his every request. The young prince had never gotten over the thrill of being able to communicate with the King, and he often sent messages of thanksgiving and adoration, as well as the usual requests for help in time of need.

Josiah nodded at Sir Faithful's words. "I will make frequent use of my right as a son of the King. I will send frequent petitions to His Majesty."

The old man stepped close and wrapped his arms around the boy. "Farewell, Prince Josiah. I love you like my own son." He ran a trembling hand over his beard and then continued. "Follow the guidance of the book, lad, and listen to the voice of the dove. Be sure to send a petition to His Majesty whenever the need arises, and you will find that his resources will meet your every need. Go in faith, my prince, and you shall have a prosperous journey. Your quest will not be easy, and at times it will be utterly perilous, but King Emmanuel would not lay a burden upon you that you cannot bear. Farewell, my son. May King Emmanuel's love go with you."

Josiah returned the embrace. "Farewell, Sir Faithful. I shall miss you, but I gladly undertake this quest for my King. This time I shall not fail him."

Three hours later, Josiah climbed up on a huge boulder of granite that jutted out over the mountain trail. As he sat down to rest he drew a flask of water from the pack upon his back. Leaning back against the rock, he took a long, satisfying drink. He had been traveling through rugged territory, but he estimated that the Castle of Faith was already more than sixty furlongs behind him. Glancing up into the boughs of a giant oak that shaded the boulder upon which he sat, he caught a glimpse of the dove.

The book had guided him to this point. He had been careful to follow the map he found within its pages, and each time he came to a fork in the trail or a juncture where another trail or road intersected the Path of Righteousness, he simply opened the book and let it guide him. He had found that the pages of the book glowed with a soft light whenever he turned down the right path, but dimmed when he took a wrong turn. Thus, he learned to consult the book each and every time he had a decision to make.

Looking down from his position atop the granite boulder he could see below him a series of wooded hills that fell away before him like stairs. The Path of Righteousness wound its way down the side of the hill upon which he sat and disappeared over the crest of the nearest ridge, then reappeared on a slope in the distance. As he studied the countryside below him, he spotted a second trail, and then a third and a fourth. *I'll have to use the book very carefully when I get down there,* he told himself, *so I don't end up following the wrong trail.*

A twig broke with a loud snap just below the boulder, and Josiah looked down to see a tall man dressed in blue and yellow standing in the path at the base of the giant rock. "Greetings, fellow traveler!" the stranger hailed him. "And to which destination might your steps be taking you?"

"I'm on a quest to the Castle of Virtue," Josiah replied. "King Emmanuel sent me."

The man smiled and nodded in a friendly way. "I've been there many times myself," he told Josiah. "Might I show you a shortcut? It would save you a furlong or two of walking and hasten you on your way."

"Don't listen to him," a still, small voice warned, but Josiah didn't hear.

"Do you see the village at the base of yon hill? Pass through that village and then follow the road that leads to the east. You will find yourself at the gates of the Castle of Virtue within two hours."

"What village is that I see?" Josiah asked, gazing at the small cluster of yellow thatched rooftops in the distance. "Are the inhabitants loyal to King Emmanuel?"

The man shrugged. "I wouldn't worry about the loyalties of the Littlekins," he replied casually. "The villagers are so small that they couldn't cause you much grief even if they set out to directly oppose you. They're quite harmless. Take my word for it, lad, the path through the village is by far the best route."

"Are you certain, sire?" Josiah questioned. "My book said nothing about a shortcut to the Castle of Virtue." He watched the stranger closely. The man's voice seemed familiar, but Josiah was quite certain he had never seen the man before.

"Trust my experience, lad," the man challenged. "I am a candlemaker by trade, and I have made many trips to the Castle of Virtue to sell my wares. This is by far the shortest and easiest route." He lifted one hand in a casual wave. "Farewell, my friend, and have a pleasant journey." Sauntering down the trail, he soon disappeared from view among the trees.

Josiah thought it over. If the friendly candlemaker were a frequent traveler in this part of the kingdom, would he not be wise to take the man's advice? And if the shortcut to the Castle of Virtue would save him time and trouble, would it not be in his best interests to follow it? A tiny, disquieting doubt nagged at him, but he quickly pushed it to the back of his mind and did his best to ignore it. He took another long drink from the flask, shoved it back into his backpack, and stood to his feet.

His mind was made up—he would follow the advice of the helpful stranger.

Three minutes later he was surprised to find himself nearing the little village that he had seen from the hillside. Apparently, the town was much closer than it had appeared from his vantage on the boulder. A whitewashed sign at the side of the trail proclaimed in bold letters, "Welcome, traveler, to the Village of the Littlekins."

As he entered the Village of the Littlekins he stopped and stared around in astonishment. Both sides of the narrow street were lined with tiny cottages that were barely higher than his waist! He knelt in the street and studied the strange little buildings. "Who lives in these tiny houses?" he wondered aloud. "They're so small—they must have been built for rabbits!"

Reaching out to touch one little house, he lifted a tiny latch and opened a little door barely fourteen inches high. He knelt down and peered in through the tiny doorway. A small fire blazed merrily in a miniature fireplace less than twelve inches wide, and a cooking pot the size of a teacup hung over the flames, bubbling and steaming and filling the tiny chamber with a delicious aroma. Tipping his head to one side, he studied the interior of the little house, noting with amazement the little bed in one corner, the tiny benches, and the little table too small to hold a single roast goose.

Whoever lives here is hardly as tall as a chicken, Josiah told himself. *I've never seen such a tiny house! Perhaps these little houses were built for rabbits, or squirrels, or raccoons or badgers... no, raccoons and badgers would be too large to live here.* It appeared that the occupants of the tiny cottage were not at home, so he quietly closed the little door.

Still on his hands and knees, Josiah opened the door of the next little house and peered in. A piercing scream issued from within the little dwelling. Startled, he quickly closed the little door. He shook his head in astonishment. In the brief instant that he had looked inside the little house, he had seen two women down on their knees at a washtub filled with suds, vigorously scrubbing homespun garments. But the women were hardly as big as three-week-old kittens!

He leaned close and tried to peer in the tiny window, hoping for another glimpse of the little women. However, the sunlight reflected off the glass and all he could see was his own reflection. But he did hear more screams from inside the cottage.

Afraid that he had upset the mistress of the little house, Josiah turned and hurried back the way he had come until he was safely out of the strange little village. He saw a small stream by the side of the road, so he hurried down to it to refill his flask and take a drink. After he had refreshed himself he sat down on a fallen log on the creek bank to think matters through. He had seen no one in the strange little village—except for the unbelievably tiny women that he had frightened by peeking in the little door—but he felt uneasy just passing through.

The candlemaker said that this was the best route, he told himself. *If the Littlekins are all as small as those two tiny women are, what is there to be afraid of?* But he still couldn't dismiss the uneasy feeling inside. He couldn't explain it, but something inside told him that he was in great danger. He took a deep breath. *I'll just get to my feet and walk right through that tiny village!* he decided. *What can happen?*

"A thousand pardons, my lord," a tiny voice said, interrupting his thoughts, "but would you be so kind as to allow me to take a seat on this log?"

Josiah stared, hardly able to believe his eyes. Standing before him was a tiny little imp of a man dressed in a green jerkin and brown leggings. The little man was slightly less than a foot tall, with spindly legs and arms and a curly, brown beard. "Who are you?" the young prince gasped in astonishment. "Where did you come from?"

"My name is Envy," the wee little man said, scratching at his beard with fingers hardly bigger than grains of rice. "I'm from the village."

"The Village of the Littlekins?"

The little man nodded proudly. "Aye."

"Then you must be a Littlekin," Josiah ventured, still trying to recover from the surprise of seeing a third adult too small to even reach his knee.

"Indeed, I am, my lord," Envy replied. He gestured toward the log with a tiny hand. "May I?"

"Certainly," Josiah responded. The man's name sounded ominous, and he had a certain crafty look about him, but he was such a little fellow that Josiah could not see how he could possibly do any harm. Envy took a flying leap, grasped the top of the log, and pulled himself up on top.

The little man had hardly settled himself on the log beside Josiah when another little man about the same size appeared. The newcomer was dressed much as the first, except that his jerkin was pale blue. "My lord, this is a friend of mine," Envy said, eyeing Josiah carefully. "His name is Greed. Would you mind greatly if he were to rest on the log for a spell?"

"Aye, there's plenty of room," Josiah replied, studying the two little men with curiosity. Greed quickly made himself comfortable on the log.

Scarcely a minute had passed when Josiah looked over to see a third tiny man hiking through the underbrush and heading straight for the log. "Who are you?" Josiah asked. "I suppose that you would want a seat on the log, too."

"My name is Discontent," the tiny man replied. "If it's no trouble, my lord, indeed I would like to rest a bit." He was dressed in solid brown, and had a thin face and dark, beady eyes, which gave him a striking resemblance to a rat. Discontent clambered up onto the log and took a seat beside the first two tiny men.

Ten minutes later, the log was crowded. Twelve tiny men, not one of whom was tall enough to reach to Josiah's knee, were seated on the log beside the young prince. Josiah studied the group of Littlekins. For the most part they were dirty and rough and uncouth, with gruff countenances and surly manners, quite different from the polite civility of the first visitor, Envy. They argued with one another, pushing and shoving and knocking each other off the log and in general becoming quite obnoxious. Their language was atrocious, and Josiah began to feel very uncomfortable, even to the point that he began to wish that he had not allowed Envy to take a seat on the log in the first place.

Josiah noticed that from time to time the little men whispered to each other and eyed him as though they were plotting mischief against him. He felt no fear, since the men were so much smaller than he. *They probably don't weigh more than two or three pounds apiece,* he told himself.

"Hey, big one, make a little more room," a foul smelling little man named Idleness growled at Josiah.

The young prince tried to scoot over just a trifle, but the Littlekin on the other side of him let out a squeal of rage. "Clumsy ox! Watch what you are doing! Keep to yourself! You have nearly squashed me!" He beat against Josiah's leg with his tiny fists.

"I beg your pardon," Josiah muttered, reminding himself that he had taken a seat on the log before any of these tiny men and wondering if he should bring the matter up.

"You are taking entirely too much room," a plump Littlekin named Gluttony declared a moment later, glaring accusingly at Josiah.

"We will have to ask you to get down," another added.

Josiah laughed. "I was here first. It's my log. You are sitting here at my permission."

Josiah's words provoked a chorus of angry muttering. The Littlekins became violently angry and actually began to attempt to push Josiah off the log! The boy laughed as he pushed back. "You cannot hurt me," he taunted. "You are but a swarm of grasshoppers!"

One of the little men leaped to his feet and blew a long blast on a hunting horn. The sound reverberated through the trees. Suddenly becoming aware of the clamor of angry voices, Josiah turned to see a horde of tiny townspeople rushing through the woods straight toward him. The men were carrying pitchforks, shovels, hayrakes and hoes; the women had rolling pins, brooms and other assorted weapons, and it was obvious that the furious inhabitants of the little town meant to do him harm. "It's one of the big 'uns!" a man's voice shouted. "Get 'im!"

Josiah leaped to his feet, but he was not alarmed in the least. The biggest man in the crowd was barely twelve inches tall. The angry horde of Littlekins swarmed around Josiah's ankles, stabbing and striking at his feet and lower legs with their tiny makeshift weapons. Josiah laughed. The little people were attacking him in fury, but their assaults felt like pinpricks. *With one good kick I could send thirty of them flying,* he told himself in amusement.

"Little folk, what are you doing?" he cried, doing his best to hold back his laughter at the absurdity of the assault. To him, the attack of the little people seemed as frivolous as a pack of mice attacking a lion. "I'm not your enemy!"

The angry horde swelled in numbers until the clearing was filled with tiny villagers. Shouting and screaming in their tiny voices, they surged forward, competing with each other for the opportunity to take a swing at the amused young prince. But their furious assault was having little effect; Josiah could hardly feel their feeble blows. "Kill him!" the Littlekins screamed to each other. "Envy, kill him! Discontent, chop his toes off! Laziness, slice his ankles to ribbons!"

Josiah took a step backwards, stumbling over some of the little people and knocking them flat, though he managed to avoid stepping on any of them. The tiny villagers responded in a blind rage, swarming forward like a colony of oversized ants and screaming in their eagerness to do him harm. Swinging their tiny weapons, they battered his knees, shins and ankles with all their might. Josiah was doubled over with laughter at the absurdity of the situation. The attack of the Littlekins was having little effect upon him, but a good many of their furious blows were falling on each other, with telling results.

One brave young villager had ventured to scramble up into a thin sapling. He launched himself at Josiah, managed to catch hold of Josiah's belt, and hung on for dear life. Josiah brushed his tiny attacker away, doing his best not to hurt the little man.

"I am not your enemy!" the young prince called again, trying to reason with the horde of angry little people. "I'm just passing through on my way to the Castle of Virtue. Please stop! I do not wish to harm any of you."

But his words fell on deaf ears. The angry mob of Littlekins now numbered in the hundreds. They surged forward, shouting and swinging and pressing against his shins until he was compelled to take several steps backwards. Suddenly his boots caught and he found himself falling backwards. Two of the Littlekins had strung a rope between two trees and managed to trip him. As he hit the ground, the mob shouted exultantly and swarmed over him like ants on a dead grasshopper.

Prince Josiah still was not alarmed as he rolled over and leaped to his feet. If it was a fight that these Littlekins wanted, then it was a fight they were going to get! But somehow the frantic hordes of tiny villagers had managed to throw a noose around his neck, and, as he attempted to stand up, they jerked him down into the dust again. Josiah lunged upward against the tiny rope, flinging dozens of little people to the ground like so many toy dolls. He struggled to his knees, but the Littlekins pulled him to the ground again by the sheer weight of their numbers.

"Get off me!" Josiah shouted, struggling and thrashing about in a desperate attempt to free himself. "Let go of me!" He threw his arms wide, scattering Littlekins left and right. Throwing his hands to his neck, he grasped the noose about his throat and attempted to pull it open. The Littlekins swarmed over him again, shouting and kicking and hitting him.

Realizing for the first time the seriousness of the situation that he was in, Josiah pulled the book from his doublet and swung it mightily. In an instant the little black volume became a two-edged sword. The Littlekins leaped back in fright as the glittering blade sliced through the air. Josiah advanced slowly, swinging the sword with all his might. The tiny villagers retreated before him, squealing with fright as they scattered like autumn leaves before a gust of wind. He gave a tremendous sigh of relief when he saw how easily the Littlekins could be put to flight.

At that moment a heavy weight came crashing down on the back of his head. Josiah saw a brilliant flash of white light explode inside his head. The sword fell from his hand. Darkness descended abruptly.

Chapter Three

Prince Josiah awoke to find that he was lying in the shade of a giant oak. When he tried to move he discovered that his hands were tightly bound behind him. The Littlekins were swarming about him, dancing up and down in delight as they celebrated their capture of such a large prisoner.

Josiah rolled over and attempted to struggle to his feet, but the noose around his neck brought him crashing to the ground. The Littlekins had him firmly under their control.

The crowd of Littlekins abruptly parted. A small company of soldiers came dashing up with tiny swords drawn, stopping just inches from Josiah's face. Smartly dressed in red doublets with gold braid, white leggings, and shiny black boots, the pint-size soldiers were under the command of a stern-faced officer by the name of Captain Temptation. "On your feet, prisoner!" the captain roared, holding the point of his tiny sword against the tip of Josiah's nose. "On your feet, before I run you through!"

The young prince rolled over and struggled to his knees. Though his hands were bound behind him, he glanced around desperately for his sword. He caught a glimpse of three red-uniformed troops struggling under the weight of the weapon as they carried it through the trees. "Come back with that!"

Josiah shouted. His heart sank. Without the sword he was helpless—even against his tiny captors—and he knew it.

"On your feet, prisoner!" Captain Temptation ordered again. Josiah sighed and grudgingly obeyed.

The villagers had formed a double line, each with a firm grip on the long rope that terminated in the noose around his neck, and now they began to pull him toward the village. Tiny as they were, their combined weight and strength was too much for the young prince, and he was forced to follow meekly along. *They caught me off guard*, Josiah berated himself. *If I had been alert and watchful, this would never have happened. It all started when I allowed Envy to take a place beside me on the log.*

He looked down at the tiny captain who was marching proudly alongside his prisoner. "Where are you taking me?"

"You must stand before our magistrate, Lord Careless," Captain Temptation replied, "to answer the charges against you."

"What charges?" Josiah demanded.

"You will find out when Lord Careless deals with you," the tiny soldier answered, giving Josiah a disgusted look. "Now move along quietly."

The triumphant Littlekins proudly paraded their prisoner through the narrow streets of their tiny village, laughing and chattering as they marched along. Josiah shuffled through the lanes with his head down, overwhelmed at the suddenness of his capture. *I have failed again,* he thought bitterly. *I have failed King Emmanuel! But the Littlekins are so tiny. Who would have thought that there were so many of them, or that they could fight so efficiently?* Remorse filled his soul. *I should never have allowed Envy to take a place on the log, even though he is so tiny. Once again, I have failed my King! I should never have listened to the candlemaker and detoured through the village of the Littlekins!*

The procession reached the center of the village and approached a large building with stately pillars and marble steps. Josiah stared at the massive building which seemed so out of place among the tiny dwellings. As the Littlekins led him up the steps, a growing sense of dread overwhelmed him. *So this is the Courthouse—the place where I will stand before Lord Careless.*

Once inside the building, the Littlekins abandoned their places on the rope and scattered to find seats, leaving Josiah in the charge of Captain Temptation and his company of tiny soldiers. Even though there were only ten or twelve of the pint-size troops and Josiah could easily have overpowered several times that many, he was too discouraged and defeated to even try to resist. Meekly he allowed himself to be led to the front of the crowded courtroom.

A tiny, gray-haired bailiff with a large, droopy mustache stood upon a raised platform at the front of the courtroom. "Court is now in session," he cried in the loudest voice he could muster, "with the Honorable Lord Careless presiding. All rise!"

The throng of noisy Littlekins jumped to their feet and a hush fell over the room. A dignified Littlekin wearing a long black robe entered through a side door. Upon his head was a powdered wig. Even before the magistrate walked to the raised desk in the center of the platform, Josiah knew that the robed figure was the Honorable Lord Careless.

"Be seated," Lord Careless said in a flat, toneless voice. "Defendant, approach the bench."

Josiah was standing directly in front of the platform—so close that he could have reached out and touched the desk—so he merely raised his eyes and looked at Lord Careless.

"The defendant will approach the bench!" Lord Careless declared loudly. His voice was still flat and lifeless, but his eyes flashed with anger. Josiah inched half a step closer. "That's better," the magistrate declared. "By what name are you called?"

"Prince Josiah of the Castle of Faith, Your Honor."

The magistrate unrolled a parchment and studied it in silence for half a minute. Then he leaned over and looked down at Josiah. "Does the defendant understand these charges against him?"

"Your Honor, I have not even heard the charges," the young prince replied. "What are they?"

"Do you understand the charges against you?" Lord Careless demanded sharply. Usually it is quite difficult to speak sharply in a monotone, but the tiny magistrate managed it quite nicely.

"Sire, what are the charges?" Josiah asked again.

"Just answer the question," the magistrate snapped irritably, as though he was already tired of the affair, though the court had just been called into session.

"Nay, sire, I do not understand the charges," Josiah asserted, "for I have not yet heard them. And I don't understand why your people have arrested me, for I was merely planning to pass through your village without harming—"

"Silence!" Lord Careless roared, a remarkable feat for a man his size. He snatched the parchment from his desk and thrust it at the bailiff. "Read the charges."

"Aye, my lord." The bailiff held the document up in front of his face and began to read. "The people of the Village versus the giant stranger, Prince Josiah. The prince is charged with trespassing, entering our village with malicious intent to harm, creating a disturbance, malicious assault, maligning the citizenry, inciting a riot, and resisting arrest." He rolled the parchment up and handed it back to Lord Careless.

"That's ridiculous!" Josiah protested. "I didn't do any of those things!"

"One last charge, Your Honor," the bailiff said, taking the parchment and scribbling something upon it. "Contempt of court."

"How do you plead?" Lord Careless asked, taking the parchment from the bailiff.

"Guilty!" the entire crowd of Littlekins cried with one voice, before Josiah could even open his mouth.

"A guilty plea has been entered," Lord Careless told the bailiff, handing the parchment back to him. The bailiff promptly recorded it on the document.

"Wait!" Josiah cried in desperation. "That wasn't me—I didn't say anything! I'm not guilty! These charges are completely false, and they cannot prove any of them against me!"

Lord Careless turned and looked at Captain Temptation, who stood stiffly at attention with his company of red-uniformed soldiers in one corner of the courtroom. "Can these charges be proven, Captain?"

"Aye, Your Honor." The little captain turned and called, "Bring in the evidence!"

Three soldiers entered the courtroom through the side door, bearing Josiah's sword over their heads as they entered. The crowd of Littlekins gasped at the sight of the weapon as though they had never seen it before. Lord Careless rose from his seat, leaned over the bench, and stared down at the sword. "What is this, Captain?"

"It's an instrument of death, Your Honor. We found it in the possession of the defendant and took it from him by force." The captain turned and addressed the three soldiers. "Permit Lord Careless to examine the evidence."

The tiny soldiers carried Josiah's sword up onto the platform. Grunting with the effort, they placed the hilt of the weapon against the floor and raised the blade vertically into the air. A murmur of excitement swept through the crowd of spectators. Lord Careless shook his head gravely as though he were appalled at the sight of such a fierce weapon.

"Beware!" The sword began to lean dangerously to one side and the three little soldiers suddenly lost control of it. All three leaped to safety, allowing the weapon to fall unimpeded. The blade flashed in a long silver arc as it fell, slicing down upon the desk just inches from Lord Careless with such force that it cut the wooden desktop cleanly in two. The startled magistrate toppled backwards off his seat, losing his wig in the process.

"Fools! Fools, every one of you!" Lord Careless glared at the three soldiers as he rose from the floor and took his seat behind the desk, unaware of the fact that his bald head now glistened in the sunlight from the courtroom windows.

The crowd of Littlekins had shrunk back in fear as the sword fell, and then burst into laughter when their magistrate lost his seat. When he reappeared moments later without his wig, their laughter turned into uncontrolled howls of merriment. In spite of the predicament he was in, Prince Josiah joined in their laughter.

"Silence!" Lord Careless slammed his gavel down upon the ruined desk, still unaware of the missing hairpiece. "Order in the court! Silence!" The laughter continued, swelling in volume until it filled the courtroom. The Littlekins howled with mirth, holding their sides and wiping their eyes. They couldn't have stopped laughing even if they had wanted.

Lord Careless was furious. He banged the gavel repeatedly. "Order! Order!" he screamed, hopping up and down in his rage. "I will have order in this court!" The laughter continued, unchecked and unrestrained. Helpless to stop it, the tiny magistrate turned on his assistant. "Bailiff! Restore this courtroom to order!"

The bailiff was struggling to hold back his own laughter as he hurried to the desk, retrieved Lord Careless' wig from the floor behind him, and plopped it unceremoniously upon the magistrate's bald head. The laughter in the courtroom reached a crescendo.

The proud magistrate was thoroughly humiliated. "Silence!" he screamed, pounding the splintered desk so furiously that the head of the gavel separated from the handle and flew across the courtroom to strike an elderly Littlekin upon the shoulder. "I will have order!"

A hush fell across the courtroom as swiftly as a cloud blots out the sun. Lord Careless eyed the ruined gavel for several long seconds and then studied the remains of the desk. The three soldiers cowered in fear.

"One final charge," the magistrate growled, biting off the end of each word as he glared furiously at Josiah. "Destruction of village property!"

The frightened young prince looked around the courtroom in desperation, for there was no question that Lord Careless and the tiny inhabitants of the Village of the Littlekins had determined evil against him. He looked beseechingly to the back of the courtroom at Envy, the Littlekin who had first approached him so politely, but the little man glared back as maliciously as the rest of the villagers. Josiah realized that there was nothing he could do—his hands were securely bound and the noose was still around his neck. He was at the mercy of the court.

"Stand and be sentenced!" Lord Careless ordered. Josiah was already standing, but he knew now that the tiny magistrate expected a response, so he simply leaned closer to the bench. His head slumped in defeat.

"Your malicious crimes against the citizenry of this village are numerous and of great magnitude. I hereby sentence you"—Lord Careless paused and Josiah winced—"to a duel between you and any male citizen of your choosing."

"A duel?" Josiah's head shot up. "What kind of a duel?"

"A test of strength," the magistrate replied. "A contest of force. You are to engage in a wrestling match. If you shall win, you shall go free. But if you lose, you are our slave forever."

"But, sire, I am not guilty!" Josiah protested.

"Select your opponent."

"I am to choose, Your Honor?"

"Select any male citizen of this village," the magistrate repeated slowly, as if irritated at Josiah's dullness. "You will wrestle him. If you can prevail, you are free; but if you shall lose, you are our slave forever."

An expectant hush fell over the crowd as Josiah gazed around the courtroom. *I can whip any ten of these puny little men,* Josiah thought scornfully. *I can whip twenty, or thirty! Lord Careless must not realize just whom he is dealing with here.* His gaze fell upon Envy. *He's the one responsible for this whole predicament,* Josiah thought angrily. *I'll squash him like a bug! His arms are about as thick as my little finger!*

He turned to face Lord Careless. "I choose Envy."

"Envy?" The magistrate addressed the tiny man. "Do you accept the challenge?"

Envy stood to his feet. "With pleasure, Your Honor."

"Unbind the defendant," Lord Careless ordered, and Captain Temptation stepped forward to carry out the order. Josiah knelt so that the tiny soldier could reach the ropes. In no time, his hands were free and the noose was removed from around his neck.

He stood to his feet and watched Envy as he strode confidently forward. A leering grin was on his tiny face, and he flexed his skinny arms, almost as if he expected to win the match. Josiah shook his head in disbelief. *I'm more than five times as tall as he is! I weigh fifty times as much as he does! Doesn't this little fellow realize what he is up against?*

Josiah began to relax. *This won't be so difficult after all. Once I beat this skinny little runt, I'll leave the Village of the Littlekins behind me and continue with my journey to the Castle of Virtue. I can't lose against such a puny adversary.*

As the grinning Littlekin marched toward the front of the courtroom to accept the challenge, Josiah's mouth dropped open. He stared in dismay. With each step he took, Envy was growing a little larger. He was halfway down the aisle and already he was nearly five feet tall. By the time he reached the front of the room, the tiny Littlekin had become a hulking giant of a man, more than eight feet tall, with huge arms and shoulders that bulged with powerful muscles!

Seizing the terrified prince by the throat, the enormous Littlekin lifted him off the floor with one hand. "I accept the challenge, Your Honor," he growled in a deep voice that reverberated like thunder throughout the courtroom. "Aye, I look forward to it!" He relaxed his grip and allowed the boy to sink to the floor.

Overcome with fear, Josiah rose slowly to his feet. If he lost the match against his gigantic adversary, he was to be the slave of the Littlekins forever. He trembled at the thought.

Chapter Four

"The match will now begin," Lord Careless announced. "Envy, loyal resident of our village, will combat the defendant, Prince Josiah, of the Castle of Faith. If the defendant wins the match he will be acquitted of the charges against him. If Envy wins the match, the defendant becomes our slave forever."

Eager to fight the young prince, Envy leaned forward with a cruel leer on his features. Josiah's heart pounded with fear. Just moments before the Littlekin had been a tiny man less than a foot tall, but now he was well over nine feet. The crowded courtroom was filled with the chants of the excited villagers. "Envy! Envy! Envy!"

Prince Josiah was desperate. He quickly scanned the courtroom, frantically seeking a way out of his dilemma, but the exits were blocked with throngs of Littlekins eager to witness the duel. He glanced back at Envy. His hulking adversary was growing faster and faster and was now more than ten feet tall! Completely overcome with terror, Josiah backed away.

The huge Littlekin grinned smugly as he took a menacing step forward. "Come to me, Prince Josiah of the Castle of Faith," he taunted, beckoning with his thick, hairy hands. "I shall show you a thing or two!"

"King Emmanuel, I desperately need your help," Josiah whispered. Fear swept over him in waves and his chest felt so tight that he could scarcely breathe. His trembling legs seemed ready to give way at any moment. *A petition! I must send a petition to His Majesty!* Lacking a parchment to write upon, the young prince snatched the rolled document from the hands of the startled bailiff. *I don't have time to put my petition into words,* he thought frantically. *I just hope that King Emmanuel will understand my unspoken plea!*

"A petition to my King," he said softly, holding the rolled parchment aloft. He released it, and to his relief, the petition shot from his hand and vanished from the courtroom.

"What manner of craftiness is this?" Lord Careless demanded, leaning across the bench and glaring at Josiah. A murmur of angry Littlekin voices swept across the crowded courtroom. Captain Temptation and his red-uniformed troops drew their swords and started forward.

"Use your sword," a still, small voice prompted, and in the midst of his confusion and terror, Josiah heard. He looked up. The dove was perched on the chandelier directly over the magistrate's bench. "Use your sword. His Majesty's power is found within your sword."

Josiah nodded. What was it that Sir Faithful had said when speaking of the dove? *"Obedience to his voice will guarantee success in your quest for the seven castles."* The sword! Where was it?

The royal sword lay across the splintered desk within reach of Lord Careless. Josiah leaped to the platform, seized the weapon, and whirled about to confront Envy. He sprang directly at the gigantic Littlekin, swinging the invincible weapon with all his might. The suddenness of the move caught Envy by surprise, and he leaped back to evade the blade. Encouraged, the young prince charged forward, swinging the sword furiously.

Cowed by the threat of the glittering sword, Envy retreated, stumbling backward over the masses of Littlekins huddled behind him. He struggled to regain his balance and then tumbled to the courtroom floor with a resounding crash as the terrified Littlekins leaped in all directions to avoid being crushed by the enormous bulk. Shrieks of outrage filled the courtroom.

Quick to follow through with his momentary advantage, Josiah whirled and dashed to the door at the opposite side of the courtroom. Littlekins blocked the way, but Josiah's sword sliced left and right with lightning swiftness. With shrieks of terror the tiny villagers scattered like chaff before the wind. Captain Temptation and his tiny soldiers were nowhere in sight. Josiah dashed through the door, slamming it behind him.

"Follow me!" a small voice called, and the young prince turned in time to see the dove dart into the shadows of the forest behind the courthouse. Josiah plunged into the dense woods and ran as hard as he could.

He caught a glimpse of the dove's beautiful white plumage and dashed in that direction. Following the flight of the dove, he soon came to a moss-covered cabin. An elderly man stood before the cabin door as if waiting for him. "Come in hither, my prince," the man called as Josiah came in sight. "You shall be safe with me!" The dove darted into the cabin, so Josiah felt that it was safe to follow. The man stepped in behind him and closed the door.

"I must hide!" Josiah blurted, breathing hard. "The Littlekins will soon be here!"

The old man turned slowly. His face was calm and peaceful and his clear gray eyes sparkled with friendliness. "The Little Sins will not venture to pursue you, Prince Josiah," he replied softly. "They fear the power of your sword."

Josiah stared at the old man. "Little Sins?" he echoed. "But sire, they are called the 'Littlekins'. I saw it on the sign at the entrance to their village!"

"Little Sins," the cabin owner corrected gently. "You have misread the sign." He shook his grizzled head sadly. "Many a child of the King has been caught off guard by the Little Sins, as you were today. Envy, Gluttony, Pride, Apathy, Greed—they all seem so small and so harmless, but once they are allowed to abide in the human heart, they quickly take over. The Little Sins are often just as deadly adversaries as the transgressions that we would consider the 'Big Sins.' "

Josiah nodded and held his sword against his side. When it changed into the book, he thrust it carefully inside his doublet. "They nearly conquered me," he said in agreement. "They wanted to make me a slave forever." He paused and looked at the old man in bewilderment. "Sire, how did you know my name?"

"I am a nobleman in the service of King Emmanuel. My name is Sir Wisdom. I was sent here to help you on your journey to the Castle of Virtue. As you have learned already, there will be many obstacles for you to overcome before you can reach the castle."

"I shouldn't have tried to pass through the Village of the Little Sins," Josiah said contritely. "My book did not guide me there, and yet I ventured on that path."

Sir Wisdom smiled sadly. "Aye, you were tricked," he explained, "by your old pal, Palaois Anthropos."

"My old nature?" Josiah was shocked. "But this man was a candlemaker, sire, not a tinker, as Palaois Anthropos was. And he didn't look like..."

"Palaois can be quite crafty. I warn you—you have not seen the last of him." The old man led Josiah to a small table, upon which two bowls of steaming porridge were set. A cheerful fire crackled upon the hearth. "You must spend the night here, lad. On the morrow you will resume your journey to the Castle of Virtue. You will face three tests of your integrity, which will be three challenges to your virtue. When you have passed these three trials, you will arrive at the castle."

"Has King Emmanuel planned these trials for me?"

Sir Wisdom shook his head. "Actually, they are traps planned by your adversary, Argamor. But King Emmanuel has allowed them to take place on your journey as tests of your integrity, and they can become the means of growth. Remember, Prince Josiah, Argamor can only place obstacles in your path if King Emmanuel allows them."

Josiah pulled up a stool and sat down at the table. "Thank you, sire. Your words are an encouragement to me. Tell me, sire, what kind of trials will they be?"

"I cannot tell you, Prince Josiah. But I may tell you this—use your book and listen for the voice of the dove. Send a petition to Emmanuel whenever you encounter resistance. You must conquer your adversaries in faith—faith in your King. Then and only then shall you taste the sweetness of victory."

"Aye, that's why I failed today and was captured by the Little Sins," Josiah said with bowed head. "I didn't listen to the dove or use the book until it was almost too late. If I hadn't sent a petition to His Majesty, Envy would have prevailed, and I would have become the slave of the Little Sins forever!"

"Aye, my prince, you are learning." His host smiled gently. "Eat your porridge."

The sun was already hot upon the roadway when Prince Josiah trudged over a gentle rise and descended the winding track to the valley below. Feathery stands of pine and spruce bordered both sides of the narrow roadway. It had scarcely been half an hour since he had left Sir Wisdom's cabin after a hearty breakfast and another admonition to beware of Argamor's traps and, above all, to heed the book and obey the voice of the dove. The young prince was encouraged by the old man's reminder that King Emmanuel would never allow Argamor to place anything in his path that he could not overcome by faith and obedience to the voice of the dove. *I will send a petition to King Emmanuel at the first sign of trouble,* he reminded himself.

Josiah paused at the sight of a narrow, windswept canyon that crossed the Path of Righteousness. He crept carefully to the edge and looked down. Far below, a swift river pounded and surged over rocks and boulders as it raced madly along in its quest for the sea. The thunderous roar of the water flowing through the narrow canyon and the white spray that flew in the air above the rocks testified of the restless power of the swift current. Clearly, this was not the place to ford the river.

He studied the canyon itself. The gray stone walls fell away abruptly in a rugged series of crags and crevices that were far too treacherous for a human to scale. There had to be another way across. As the young prince stood silently pondering his predicament, a shower of small rocks rattled down the slope and fell over the precipice to disappear into the chasm below. Startled, Josiah looked up to realize that something or someone had journeyed down the trail and passed by before he even knew that he was not alone.

Prince Josiah scrambled back up to the trail and hurried to catch up with the traveler. "Wait!" he called. But the man or beast or whatever it was had already disappeared around a bend in the trail. Josiah ran to catch up.

He dashed around the bend just in time to see a man in

peasant's clothing follow the trail to the edge of the canyon, drop a small object into a metal container at the side of the path, and then step out onto a wooden bridge that spanned the narrow canyon. Josiah's heart leaped. A bridge! Here was a way to cross the canyon.

He paused in the middle of the trail and watched as the traveler made his way across. The bridge looked ancient; the uprights were badly weathered and the planks were splintered and decaying. In places, the planks were missing altogether, leaving gaping holes where a misstep could result in a fatal plunge to the raging river below. But the traveler crossed safely and continued on his way without mishap.

If he can do it, I can too, Josiah told himself. *He weighs half again as much as I do. If the bridge will hold him, it will most certainly hold me.* He hurried down the approach to the rickety bridge and cautiously lifted a foot to take the first step.

A strong hand against his chest restrained him from stepping out onto the bridge. "Your toll, lad. You haven't paid your toll."

Startled, Josiah glanced over to see a heavyset man in tattered brown homespun sitting on a small boulder beside the bridge. "My toll, sire?"

"Nobody crosses the bridge for naught," the man told him crossly. "The crossing will cost you a threepence."

"Threepence!" Josiah echoed. "But sire, I have no money."

The man shrugged. "This is a toll bridge, lad. Those who do not pay do not cross."

"But I am on the King's business!" Josiah protested. "I am Prince Josiah, from the Castle of Faith, and I am traveling to the Castle of Virtue. In the name of King Emmanuel I request that you would allow me to pass."

"Nay, not without a threepence," the man insisted, shrugging to indicate that it mattered not to him that Josiah was on an errand for the King. "Those who do not pay do not cross."

Perplexed, Josiah walked back up the trail. He sank to a seat on a boulder in the shade of a willow while he considered his dilemma. *I can't turn back! But the bridge appears to be the only way across, and I have no money. What am I to do?*

"There is a way across, my lord."

Josiah turned, startled, to see a wrinkled old woman sitting in the shade of the tree. The woman wore wretched, dirty clothing. Her graying hair was disheveled and matted; and when she smiled, Josiah saw that she was missing several teeth. *A gypsy,* he thought, with some alarm. But the woman was smiling in a friendly manner as she sidled toward him, and Josiah began to relax.

"There is a way across, my lord," she said again as she drew close to Josiah's boulder.

"How, my good woman? I see no other way but the bridge. The walls of the canyon are too steep, and the river cannot be forded."

"The bridge is the only way, unless one cares to walk a hundred furlongs downstream to a place where it can be forded. You must cross by way of the bridge."

"But I have no money," Josiah protested.

"Nor have I, my lord, but I cross whenever I please."

"But there is a toll collector, and he will not allow me to cross unless I drop a threepence into his kettle."

The old woman laughed. "So drop in a pebble."

"What?"

"The toll collector listens for the sound of the coin in the kettle," the old woman explained. "A pebble makes the same sound as a threepence."

Josiah was shocked. "But that would not be right! That would be dishonest!"

The woman shrugged. "The bridge does not belong to the toll collector, so he has no right to collect tolls from travelers. He did not build it, nor does he maintain it."

"Then why does he collect tolls?" Josiah asked.

"He simply laid claim to the bridge one day and began to collect tolls. No one has yet challenged him, and so he has gotten away with it."

Josiah hesitated. "But it still would not be right to deceive the toll collector by dropping in a pebble."

The old woman snorted. "I heard you say that you are on business for the King, did I not? The King's business requires haste, does it not? What would the King say if He were to learn that you have been delayed simply because you are afraid to attempt to outwit a man who is standing in the way of your success? A man who has no business collecting tolls in the first place?"

She thrust a pebble into his reluctant hand. "Go on, my lord, cross the bridge! Simply walk up, drop your pebble into the kettle, and cross the bridge as if you have paid your toll."

"I hate to be deceitful," Josiah faltered.

"Deceitful? Bah! You are merely outwitting one who stands in your way—a man who has no right to demand anything of you." Josiah still drew back, but she pushed him gently toward the bridge. "Go on! In thirty seconds you shall be safely on the other side of yon river."

The young prince took a deep breath and marched resolutely toward the sagging bridge. His heart was pounding madly as he extended a hand to drop the pebble into the kettle. The pebble made a plinking sound as it struck the bottom of the kettle, and the toll collector smiled. "Have a pleasant journey, my son." Josiah nodded, but he felt sick inside.

His heart was in his throat as he traversed the rickety structure, but he crossed the river without mishap and alighted safely on the opposite bank. He breathed a sigh of relief when he set foot on the rocky ridge above the river. He had expected to feel a sense of accomplishment when he left the bridge behind him, but instead, he felt empty and hollow inside. He had been deceitful. He tried to tell himself that he had not lied to the bridge keeper, but deep in his heart he knew that the act of tossing the pebble into the kettle in place of a coin was in reality a lie. True, he had not lied in words, but he had lied in actions. The thought troubled him.

Josiah trudged up the hill, determined to put the matter behind him. He would think of it no more. He had been deceitful, and he knew that Sir Faithful would be disappointed if he found out, but no one knew, and that was the end of the matter.

He glanced up to see an old man resting in the shade of a tall elm beside the road. As he drew closer to the traveler, he was surprised to see that it was Sir Wisdom, the old nobleman in whose cabin he had spent the night.

"Three tests, Prince Josiah," Sir Wisdom said with a mournful look and tone. "You have failed the first of the three."

Josiah's heart cried out at these words. "But sire, I could see no other way across the river! I had no money!"

"Josiah, Josiah. You are on your way to the Castle of Virtue, and yet you have used deceit to get there. What would King Emmanuel think of what you have done?"

"The old woman talked me into it," Josiah replied in a feeble attempt to defend himself, not only to Sir Wisdom, but also to his conscience, which was troubling him at that very moment. "She told me that the toll collector has no right to collect money from anyone, that he doesn't even own the bridge!"

"Who was the old woman?" the old man asked softly. "Why was she so interested in helping you across the river?"

"I don't know, sire," Josiah replied. "I guess I never wondered about it."

"Her name is Deceit, and she is an agent for Argamor, your adversary. Josiah, she was able to lead you astray because, once again, you have failed to use your book and to listen to the voice of the dove."

"But she told me that the toll collector doesn't own the bridge! That he has no right to collect money from travelers!"

"He does own the bridge," the old man replied softly, "but that's not the point. Prince Josiah, it's never right to do wrong, even if you think that you have a good reason for doing wrong."

"But how was I to get across the river?" Josiah argued.

"King Emmanuel had already provided another way, but you did not consult your book nor send a petition, and so you did not find it. This journey is a journey of faith, lad. You must learn to trust your King."

Josiah hung his head.

"There are two more tests that you must face, my young friend. Don't attempt to face them on your own. Consult your book, and listen to the voice of the dove. Then and only then you shall pass them successfully."

Sir Wisdom looked at him sadly and tenderly. "I shall go back and pay your toll, and you shall continue on your way. Prince Josiah, I wish you well. Pass these next two tests, my son. But to do so, you must use your book and listen to the voice of the dove. If you shall attempt to undertake the tests in your own strength, you shall fail again. Trust in your King, my son, and heed the book and the dove." With these words, the old nobleman was gone.

Chapter Five

With remorse in his heart, Josiah said farewell to Sir Wisdom and continued along the trail. *I failed my King again,* he thought bitterly. *How many times can I fail and still be a worthy prince, a credit to King Emmanuel? Why can I not find victory?*

The trail was growing steeper, so he used his sword to cut a thick walking staff. He marched quickly up the rocky path, fired with the energy of youth and the determination to do well in the next two tests. *I shall use my book,* he told himself resolutely, *and I shall listen for the voice of the dove. I must not fail King Emmanuel again!* Glancing upward, he caught a glimpse of the dove flitting over the treetops. Reassured, he hiked even faster.

Half an hour later Josiah came out on a shale-covered slope above a sapphire blue lake guarded by tall stands of pine, poplar, and blue spruce. The view was breathtaking. A gentle breeze whispered through the pines and scurried across the surface of the lake, kicking up tiny waves as it went, while a dancing sunbeam glittered and sparkled on the water, turning the waves into acres and acres of shimmering blue diamonds. On the far side of the lake, a tiny cabin hugged a shoreline of pure white sand.

Overhead, a lone eagle with motionless wings rode the air currents in endless circles. Josiah stood silently, transfixed by the scene before him.

He stooped and picked up a rock. As he drew his arm back to hurl the missile out over the water, his eye fell upon a small sign nearby. "***Do not throw rocks into the lake***," it said. Disappointed, he lowered his arm. "What would it hurt?" he asked himself aloud. "There's no one around, so I couldn't possibly hit anyone."

He raised the rock again, and then thought better of it. Perhaps this was the next test—he could not take that chance. He must not fail his King. Reluctantly, he opened his fingers and allowed the stone to fall into the pile of shale at his feet.

The stone bounced and rolled down the steep, shale-covered slope, picking up speed and dislodging other rocks as it traveled. Disturbed by that one stone, layers of shale began to slide downhill with a slight clattering noise. Boulders began to move, sliding slowly at first, and then rolling and tumbling and finally bouncing and leaping high into the air as they picked up speed. Soon the entire hillside below Josiah was in motion. The clatter of small tumbling rocks mingled with the grinding and jarring of large boulders and then became the thunderous roar of a gigantic rockslide.

Thousands of tons of shale and granite boulders thundered down the steep hillside to drop into the placid waters of the lake with a mighty roar and a tremendous splash. It was as if the mountain itself had fallen into the water. The result was a gigantic tidal wave taller than a tree. Josiah watched in horror as the white-crested breaker traveled across the lake with incredible speed to break upon the far shore, engulfing the tiny cabin as it crashed down with devastating force. When the wave receded, the boy could see the mangled remains of the cabin being swept down the shore. In one instant the tidal wave had reduced the secluded cabin to a pile of rubble.

Josiah stared in dismay at the spot where the tiny cabin had stood just moments before. *Did I do that? I attempted to obey the sign, but look what happened!*

Moments later a thin man in mountaineer's garb appeared at Josiah's elbow to stare in anguish at the empty beach and the debris floating in the water. "My home!" he cried, wringing his hands and swaying from side to side as if he might collapse at any moment. "My beautiful home!" He threw a pleading look at Josiah. "What happened, my lord? Did you see what happened?"

Josiah swallowed hard. "A h-huge wave s-swept it away," he croaked, choking on the words.

"Tell him the whole of the truth," his conscience demanded accusingly. *"The rock that you have dropped so carelessly caused the wave that destroyed this man's cabin! Tell him so!"*

I can't tell him that, Josiah argued. *There's no telling what he might do! And besides, I don't really know that it was my rock that caused the landslide. Perchance the entire slope was merely unstable and ready to slide into the lake, and simply happened to let loose at this particular moment.*

"It was your rock that caused the rockslide," the inner voice accused, mocking and jeering in its tone. *"You know that. Now, tell this poor man!"*

I can't! Josiah replied desperately. *I just can't!*

The mountaineer was watching him suspiciously. "My lord, did you throw a rock into the lake?" The words caught Josiah off guard.

"N-no, sire, I d-did not," Josiah stammered, truthfully enough, for he had not actually hurled the missile into the water itself. His heart smote him, for he now knew that it was he that had caused the tidal wave, even though he had not intended to. But he shrank from the idea of implicating himself.

"Do you know what caused it?" The mountaineer looked so miserable and forlorn that Josiah actually hurt inside. He swallowed hard, opened his mouth to speak, and then lost his nerve. He just couldn't bring himself to tell the grief-stricken man that he had caused the tidal wave that had destroyed his home.

Shaking his head slowly from side to side, the mountaineer sadly began to follow a narrow footpath that led down to the lake. Josiah felt miserable inside, but he just couldn't find the courage to do what he knew he ought.

"Prince Josiah, tell the poor man what actually happened."

Startled, Josiah looked over to see the dove perched in a small cherry tree beside the trail. The tree was snowy white with blossoms, rendering the celestial bird almost invisible among the branches.

"I-I can't," Josiah faltered. "I didn't intend to create the tidal wave, and I certainly didn't intend to destroy that poor man's cabin."

"You must tell him."

"I cannot. I simply cannot."

"What does your book say about this?"

At the mention of the book, Josiah suddenly realized that the entire situation he was facing was another part of the test. He must not fail. "I do not know what my book says," he replied meekly. "Where should I look?" He reached inside his doublet and withdrew the precious book.

"Open the book," the dove requested, and Josiah did so. "Turn a little further toward the back of the book." Following the dove's instructions, Josiah finally found the appropriate text. "Read it aloud."

Josiah read the passage, which spoke of providing for honest things, not only in the sight of men, but also in the sight of the King. The words struck fear into his heart. Holding the book with trembling hands, he stepped closer to the dove. "Does King Emmanuel see me right now?" he asked in a quavering voice. "Does He know what happened here?"

The dove nodded twice, spread his wings, and flew down toward the lake.

Josiah took a deep breath. He had to do what was right— he must not fail King Emmanuel again. "Wait!" he shouted, running down the winding path to catch up with the mountaineer. "There is something that I must tell you!"

Josiah glanced upward at the sky laced with buttermilk clouds, noting that he had approximately two hours of daylight remaining. "If I hurry, perhaps I can reach the Castle of Virtue before dark," he told himself aloud. "I must be getting close." Rounding a bend in the trail, he saw a small town four or five furlongs in the distance. He hastened his pace.

"Might I join you, lad?" a familiar voice called, and Josiah looked back in surprise.

"Sir Wisdom!" Josiah exclaimed. "Sire, I did not expect to see you again today!"

The old man chuckled as he hurried to catch up with Josiah. "And how did you fare in the second test, lad?"

Josiah laughed happily. "I think that you know already, but I will tell you anyway." Briefly, he recounted the events at the lake. "And the poor mountaineer was not angry with me," he told Sir Wisdom, shaking his head in relief. "He merely said that he would begin work on another cabin tomorrow. But I'm glad I told him; I felt so much better afterwards."

"That good feeling comes from doing the right thing," Sir Wisdom replied. "Now, tell me, Josiah, why did you succeed in this test when you had failed in the Village of the Little Sins, and also in the first of the three tests of integrity?"

Josiah thought it over. "Simply because this time I listened to the voice of the dove and used my book," he decided.

"Exactly! And now you know the way to victory in the third test that you must face." The old man paused in the roadway. "Well, we are almost to the town, and I must leave you here. Farewell, Prince Josiah. May I wish you success in the third test." With those words he turned and left the trail, tramping through the heather and bluebells as he headed over the side of the hill.

Josiah took a deep breath and hurried toward the town, which bustled with activity. As he entered the town gate, he spied a robust, friendly-looking vendor at the side of the narrow street. The man was standing outside his shop, attempting to call the attention of passersby to the inclined rack of baked goods in the window. A delicious aroma filled the afternoon air, and Josiah ventured over. His mouth watered at the sight of an array of fruit pastries, so fresh from the oven that they were still steaming.

"Are you traveling far, my lord?" The friendly shop owner was at his elbow, his round face beaming with interest. The tone of respect in the man's voice and the look of awe in his eyes told Josiah that the man had noticed his royal clothing, and the boy enjoyed the feeling of importance that the man's reaction produced.

"I'm on my way to the Castle of Virtue, sire."

"Just passing through, then. Would you care for a fresh apple pastry, my lord, still hot from the oven?"

"I thank you, sire, but I have no money. I expect to reach the castle before nightfall."

The shopkeeper looked around as if to be certain that no one else was within earshot and then leaned close to Josiah. "I cannot do this for everyone, my lord, but suppose I were to give you a pastry? Aye, you are hungry for one—I can see it in your eyes." Josiah opened his mouth to protest, but the eager shopkeeper was already thrusting a hot pastry into his hands. "Be on your way, my lord, and have a pleasant journey." He winked. "And not a word about this little gift, hear, or every urchin in town will be begging at my doorstep."

"I thank you, sire! You have been most kind!" The flaky pastry was almost too hot to hold. Josiah clutched it gingerly as he hurried down the narrow street, giving the tantalizing treat a moment to cool before eating it.

"Take care, knave!" A riding crop struck Josiah on the shoulder, causing him to leap back in alarm. A large sorrel mare was bearing down upon him. The rider was a fat, gaudily dressed merchant who looked extremely uncomfortable in the saddle. Instead of guiding his horse around Josiah, the man rode straight ahead. As the mare brushed past the boy, the merchant stuck out a booted foot and planted it on Josiah's chest, shoving him backwards. Josiah fell against the stone wall of a coppersmith's shop, striking his head in the process.

He leaped to his feet. "There was plenty of room for you to pass without striking me down!" he cried angrily after the departing rider. "You should watch where you are going!" The merchant ignored him and rode on.

Josiah was still seething as he brushed himself off. "There was plenty of room for him to ride around me," he muttered. "He didn't have to—" His eye fell upon an object in the street, and his anger boiled over. The apple pastry that the shopkeeper had given him was lying in the dust, and apparently the merchant's mare had stepped upon it, for it was now as flat as a sheet of parchment.

"Now look what you have done!" Josiah cried in a rage, throwing another furious glance at the fat merchant. At that moment the mare was passing through the town gate. An oxcart was entering the town from the opposite direction, and the merchant's horse sidestepped to avoid a collision, brushing against the gate as she did. A large object fell from the merchant's saddle and landed in the street, apparently unseen by the corpulent rider. The mare continued on her way.

Josiah stepped around the approaching team of oxen and ran forward to snatch up the fallen item, a large leather wallet such as travelers often used to carry supplies for their journeys. Josiah glanced around. No one was paying him any attention. He stepped to the side of the lane and opened the wallet. He found a single loaf of bread, a wedge of hard cheese, and a few brass coins—just the amount needed to purchase lodging for the night.

Josiah's mind raced. *I shall not keep the wallet, for it is not mine,* he told himself. *Aye, but suppose I just toss it under yonder bush, where no one will find it. That rude merchant will reach his destination tonight and find that he has neither food nor lodging!* The young prince laughed at the thought. *Those straits would serve him well,* he thought triumphantly, *after what he has cost me!* Glancing around, he hurried closer to the bush so that his actions would not be observed.

"What would your King have you do with the wallet?"

Josiah actually jumped in fright at the words. He looked around guiltily and was surprised to find the dove in the branches of the very bush where he intended to hide the wallet. "Did you see the way the merchant treated me?" Josiah retorted hotly. "He was too important to ride around me, and he knocked me down! And he ruined my pastry!"

"How would your King have you to respond to the rudeness of the merchant?"

This was one time when Josiah simply did not feel like listening to the voice of the dove. "The merchant ruined my pastry! I did not cause the strap on his wallet to break; the mare brushed it against the post of the gate. I owe the merchant nothing."

"Aye, but you know what your King would have you to do," the dove prodded gently. "His very words in your book are that his children are to do unto others as they would have others do unto them."

The words struck home to Josiah's heart, for he had already read that very passage one afternoon while at the Castle of Faith. He hesitated. In his imagination he could see the scornful look in the eyes of the fat merchant as he planted a boot against Josiah's chest and shoved him backwards. His anger surged anew as he remembered striking his head against the wall and as he thought of the ruined apple pastry lying in the dust. The merchant deserved no forgiveness; Josiah owed him no kindness. He drew back his hand to toss the wallet into the shadow of the bush, but paused in uncertainty.

A tall passerby spoke up at that moment. "Toss it under the bush, lad. I would not return the fat merchant's wallet. I saw what he did to you."

Josiah recognized the man's voice. "Be silent, Palaios," he said sternly, without even turning to face him. "I need no advice from you—you have caused me more than enough trouble on other occasions." Palaios retreated without further comment.

The words of the book rang in Josiah's mind and heart until he could ignore them no longer. In an instant he could see the kind, loving eyes of King Emmanuel as he reached down to break the shackles from Josiah's feet. Again he could see the fearsome scars in the King's hands.

Josiah wheeled, darted around a peasant entering the gate with a huge load of sticks upon his back, and ran after the merchant. The mare had broken into a gentle canter and the boy had to run hard to catch up with her. "Wait, sire!" he called, as he drew abreast of the horse. The merchant threw him a chilling glance and rode on. "Wait, sire, for you have lost your wallet!" Josiah shouted.

The merchant glanced again at Josiah, recognized the wallet, and immediately drew back on the reins. "Give me that!" he snarled, red-faced and angry as he leaned out of the saddle to snatch the wallet from Josiah's outstretched hand. "You little thief!"

Josiah was stunned at the man's response to his good deed. "Sire, would I be returning your wallet if I were a thief? Your mare tore it loose from your saddle when she brushed against the gate post."

In response, the merchant glared icily at Josiah and rode ahead without answering. The boy stood still in the middle of the roadway, staring in disbelief at the man's broad back. "He wasn't even grateful!" He shook his head in disappointment and disgust.

"Well done, lad! You have passed your third test!"

Startled, Josiah looked up to see Sir Wisdom approaching. The old man was beaming with delight. "You have done exactly as your King would have you do, Prince Josiah, and you have passed your test."

Josiah raised his eyebrows. "Returning that man's wallet was perhaps the hardest thing that I have ever done in my entire life. And he didn't even thank me. He treated me like a thieving street urchin."

"True, but you have listened to the dove and done as King Emmanuel would have you do, and that is all that matters. I dare say that a good part of virtue is learning to do what's right even though it is not easy and your old nature tells you to do otherwise.

"Come, lad, the Castle of Virtue is less than ten furlongs beyond the town. I will accompany you, and we shall be at the castle in less than half an hour." He put a hand on Josiah's shoulder. "The Castle of Virtue has a pastry chef who will soon make you forget all about the apple pastry that you have lost."

Chapter Six

Prince Josiah and his companion approached the Castle of Virtue just as the setting sun dropped behind the western hills. A single star hung in the platinum sky above the castle, shining white and bright like a lantern of guidance and promise. An instant later the sky darkened and a number of stars appeared as if by magic. The coming night was clear and cool, all dark shadows and silver starlight. Here and there, dark pointed firs stood half shadow and half silver while the wind whistled through their branches.

Josiah paused for a moment, gazing upward at the stars, and felt a thrill sweep over him as he found King Emmanuel's coat of arms in the constellation directly overhead. To the east, the constellation of stars formed the beautiful image of the lily of the valley. The young prince sighed with contentment and wonder. Emmanuel was Lord of the heavens as well as Lord of Terrestria.

The Castle of Virtue, a concentric stone castle very similar in appearance to the Castle of Faith, was situated high above the town on a precipitous mountainside. The approach to the gatehouse was extremely steep and difficult, and the two travelers labored hard to climb it in the purple twilight. "We're just in time," Sir Wisdom puffed. "The night is fast upon us, yet the drawbridge is still down." Their footsteps rang hollow on the wooden drawbridge as they approached the main castle gate.

"Who approaches the castle?" The challenge came from an invisible sentry in the gatehouse over their heads.

Josiah waited, but Sir Wisdom was silent, so he replied boldly, "Prince Josiah, of the Castle of Faith. With me is Sir Wisdom."

"We have been awaiting your arrival, Prince Josiah. And Sir Wisdom is always welcome at the Castle of Virtue. Advance and be recognized." Chains rattled, and the huge portcullis slowly lifted to allow them entrance. The young prince and the old man strode into the circle of torchlight illuminating the entryway.

A tall knight stepped forward to greet them. "Welcome to the Castle of Virtue," he said. "I am Sir Honesty, commander of the castle garrison. If you will follow me, I will take you to the great hall to meet Sir Honorable, the castle steward." He grinned suddenly. "Your timing is superb, my lords. Dinner is served in less than ten minutes."

Sir Wisdom smiled and winked at Josiah.

They followed Sir Honesty across the barbican, through an inner gate and across a flagstone courtyard lined with myrtle trees heavy with fragrant blossoms. A huge round moon peeked from behind a cloud just then, bathing the castle walls and courtyard with a soft silver light. A delightful feeling of accomplishment swept over Josiah. He had reached the Castle of Virtue!

The tall knight and his two guests entered an enormous room with a high, vaulted ceiling supported by massive beams. Josiah was pleased to note that the high stone walls of the great hall were adorned and brightened by colorful silk banners honoring King Emmanuel, much like the banners in the great hall at the Castle of Faith. Gazing about at the walls, he saw the familiar banners depicting the King as the Bread of Life, the Light of Terrestria, the Lily of the Valley, and many others that he had seen in the constellations in the heavens. His favorite was the banner that depicted King Emmanuel as the Great Shepherd—that one was so easy to understand. A warm feeling swept across his soul as he realized that King Emmanuel was Lord of this castle just as much as he was of the Castle of Faith. The inhabitants of this castle also loved his King.

At one end of the great hall, a huge hearth blazed brightly with a briskly snapping wood fire. Immense wrought iron chandeliers ablaze with flickering candles hung over the hall from large chains. Three rows of long trestle tables flanked by benches occupied the center of the room. King Emmanuel's table was perpendicular to the others and enjoyed a place of prominence in front of the huge fireplace. The table was ornate, set with silver service, and flanked by upholstered chairs in place of benches.

Knights and their ladies were strolling casually into the great hall, laughing and conversing warmly with each other. Squires and pages called to one another, and children laughed and chattered happily. Ladies-in-waiting exchanged greetings with members of the castle staff while servants and scullions hurried here and there, filling goblets and bearing platters of food. Attendants and pages stood at attention along the walls. A minstrel stood in one corner, frowning in concentration as he tuned the strings on his lute. In the noisy hustle and bustle of the preparation for the evening meal, the atmosphere in the great hall was one of anticipation, happiness, and contentment.

Sir Honesty led Josiah and Sir Wisdom to the King's table and instructed an attendant to seat them in places of honor. He himself took a seat immediately to Josiah's left.

A tall, broad-chested nobleman arrayed in a stunning doublet of brilliant scarlet and gold entered the great hall and strode quickly toward the King's table. Around his shoulders was a cloak of shimmering black satin; at his side swung an enormous sword with a golden hilt set with emeralds, rubies and diamonds. His rugged face was framed by a brown beard that looked incredibly soft.

Sir Honesty stood quickly to his feet as the enormous man approached the table. "Sir Honorable, allow me to introduce Prince Josiah, of the Castle of Faith. Our old friend Sir Wisdom is with him."

"Sir Wisdom, how are you?" Sir Honorable said, clapping a huge hand on the old man's shoulder in a friendly way. He turned to Josiah, and the boy saw a strong, manly face with lively brown eyes that seemed almost as kind as the eyes of King Emmanuel. "Welcome, Prince Josiah, to the Castle of Virtue," the steward said heartily. "We are honored by your presence."

"I thank you, sire," Josiah replied timidly, awed by the impressive physique of the huge nobleman. The sleeves of Sir Honorable's garment could scarcely hide the powerful muscles in the nobleman's massive arms and shoulders; the man looked as if he could single-handedly batter his way through an entire division of enemy knights.

"And how was your journey, my prince?"

Josiah glanced at Sir Wisdom before answering. "I encountered some small difficulties, sire, but I was able to overcome by using my book and heeding the voice of the dove."

The big man seemed pleased with Josiah's answer. "Well

done, my prince," he retorted, with a satisfied smile upon his handsome face.

Sir Honorable raised his hands and a hush immediately fell across the great hall. The lords and ladies, knights, squires and pages, servants, maids and children all waited attentively. The stalwart steward raised his hand, clutching a rolled parchment which Josiah knew was a petition of thanksgiving. After the petition had been sent to King Emmanuel, attendants swarmed about the tables, bearing platters of miniature meat pastries, pheasant in cinnamon sauce, beef fritters, slices of roast mutton, filets of various saltwater fish, and a vast array of colorful garden vegetables.

Josiah sighed in contentment as the servants filled the huge silver plate before him. "The food here looks every bit as good as the food at the Castle of Faith," he whispered to Sir Wisdom.

The old man smiled. "You are at His Majesty's table!" he whispered back.

Josiah sampled one of the steaming meat pastries and found it delicious. His heart filled with gratitude to his King. As the blissful inhabitants of the Castle of Virtue ate the bountiful feast that their King had provided, the minstrel strolled among the tables strumming cheerful melodies on his lute and singing many of the songs of praise that Josiah had heard at the Castle of Faith.

Josiah stayed at the Castle of Virtue for several days. Sir Honorable spent countless hours with him, teaching him just what it meant to be a man of virtue and personal integrity. Over and over he stressed the fact that a child of the King had no virtue of his own, that true virtue came from King

Emmanuel, and that Josiah would acquire virtue only as he studied and memorized his book.

"Your book tells of King Emmanuel," he would say, "and King Emmanuel is the source of all virtue. Read and study your book, Prince Josiah, and then you shall become more and more like your King. Remember that Argamor hates and fears the Word of your King, and therefore he will do all he can to keep you from your book. But if you will learn to use your book and your Shield of Faith you shall have victory over your enemy, Argamor."

Finally, the day came when Josiah was prepared to leave the Castle of Virtue and travel to his next destination, the Castle of Knowledge. Sir Honesty, Sir Honorable, and the rest of the residents of the Castle of Virtue assembled at the main gate to bid him farewell. Sir Honorable held a large emerald, which glowed with a dazzling green fire. "Lift your Shield of Faith," he told Josiah. As Josiah obeyed, the steward touched the emerald to the face of the shield, just below the coat of arms. The brilliant jewel glowed even brighter for a moment, and as Sir Honorable released it, Josiah saw that it was now permanently fused to the shield.

"May we wish you success on your journey to the Castle of Knowledge, Prince Josiah," the big castle steward called after him. "Always be a man of virtue, and serve our King faithfully!"

Sir Wisdom accompanied him to the bottom of the hill. "Farewell, my prince," he said softly. "The road to the Castle of Knowledge will not be an easy one, but you have learned the way to victory. No foe can defeat you if you will use your sword and heed the voice of the dove. You must travel this road alone, Josiah, just you and the dove, but I am assured that you will be victorious and reach the Castle of Knowledge safely. Farewell, my young friend."

With a lump in his throat Josiah bid the old man farewell and started down the road toward the Castle of Knowledge. Tilting his shield so that he could see the face of it, he admired the splendid emerald. "Six more castles to go," he whispered softly.

Chapter Seven

Prince Josiah's heart was light as he journeyed toward the Castle of Knowledge. The road was easy, with relatively few hills and slopes, and he was making good time. The furlongs fell away effortlessly beneath his feet. He had stopped for his midday meal beside a bubbling brook that seemed to sing and laugh as it traversed its rocky course. After a quick lunch of bread, mutton and cheese that the cook at the Castle of Virtue had placed in his pack, he had taken a drink from the brook and resumed his journey.

Josiah's heart overflowed with love for his King and before he even realized what was happening, a song of praise burst from his lips:

> "I once was an outcast,
> The captive of sin.
> But His Majesty found me;
> His love took me in."

The Path of Righteousness had narrowed and was now winding its way through a dense forest of cypress and mangrove trees. On his right, the pathway was bordered by a swampy bog thick with sawgrass and shaded with cypress; the knees of the giant cypress trees rose from the muck and mire like grotesque little creatures from another world. To his left, the forest was so thick and tangled that the afternoon sun pierced the gloom with only an occasional shaft of golden light. Josiah pushed ahead rapidly, unmindful of the gloominess of the region. He found himself singing the second stanza of the song of praise:

"With hands that were nail-scarred,
His Majesty came,
And broke all my shackles.
Now I praise his name!"

Hearing a slight rustle in the ferns and grasses that shrouded the roots and lower trunks of the trees on the gentle slope to his left, Josiah paused and listened. He stared hard, but could see nothing in the dense undergrowth. With a shrug, he resumed his journey. A moment later, he paused again, certain that he had heard the noise once more. It was more than just the usual animal noises one encounters when hiking in the woods; the sound seemed to be keeping pace with him as he hiked along, almost as if someone or something was stalking him. His heart pounded as he walked faster.

The rustling noise became louder, and Josiah became alarmed. Someone or something was indeed stalking him, keeping pace with him as he hurried along the trail but keeping just out of sight within the dark and gloom of the forest. At times the noise was more than just a mere rustling; whatever was stalking him was crashing through briar and bramble as loudly as a herd of cattle.

Josiah looked around for the dove, but his quiet companion was not in sight. He nervously eyed the forest, but could see nothing out of place. He walked faster yet, reaching within his doublet and drawing the book for reassurance.

The young prince gasped in fright as a knight in dark armor sprang from the trees to stand in the middle of the path.

The challenger's visor was down, obscuring his face; in his hands he held a loaded crossbow, which he pointed at Josiah's chest. "Hold your ground, rogue," the knight growled. "One more step, and I shall send a bolt through your heart!"

Josiah sucked in his breath in a long, trembling gasp. "I am Prince Josiah, heir to King Emmanuel," he said boldly, trying to keep his voice from trembling. "I am on my way to the Castle of Knowledge, and you shall not presume to stand in my way." He swung the book and the blade of steel sang through the air.

The dark knight laughed. "Come, lad, do you hope to get the best of *us*?" At the mention of the word 'us' the woods seemed to come alive as fully a dozen knights stepped from the shadows of the forest. All were armed with long bows or crossbows, which they trained upon the young prince. Their arrows and bolts were fitted with flaming tips that blazed brightly against the dark backdrop of the forest.

Josiah took a deep breath. "I am Prince Josiah, of the Castle of Faith, son and heir to King Emmanuel himself. Stand aside and let me pass."

Laughter greeted his statement. "There are thirteen of us, knave, and only one of you," the dark knight pointed out. "Surrender your sword, or we shall fill your carcass with shafts of steel."

"Never!" Josiah shouted, raising his sword and leaping forward.

The twang of bowstrings signaled Josiah's doom as the enemy soldiers released their bolts and arrows as one man. The terrified prince caught a glimpse of the flaming darts as they sped toward his heart, and he knew that this was the end. He would never reach the Castle of Knowledge.

But to his amazement, the fiery darts never reached him. The Shield of Faith on his left arm seemed to come alive as it slashed the air in front of him, deflecting every one of the enemy's fiery missiles. Through the confusion of his terror Josiah heard the sounds of the arrows and crossbolts striking steel and dimly saw the sparks and flashes as the deadly projectiles fell harmlessly to the path at his feet.

The thirteen knights gasped in astonishment as they realized that Josiah was still standing before them, unscathed and unharmed. With lightning movements they nocked their arrows and sent another fusillade of deadly missiles in his direction. Their shots, fired in haste, were wild and scattered, but just as before, the Shield of Faith deflected every bolt and arrow harmlessly to the ground.

"For the honor and glory of King Emmanuel!" Prince Josiah leaped forward, vigorously swinging the sword. With cries of terror, the enemy scattered into the woods. Within seconds, the sounds of their hasty retreat had died away and all was quiet.

The victorious young prince dropped to his knees in the middle of the path. Gripping the hilt of his invincible sword in both hands, he lowered the point of the blade to the earth and bowed his head. Moments later, he held the sword against his side until it changed into the book and then drew a parchment from within its pages and wrote a message to Emmanuel. "*I thank you, my King,*" he wrote. "*I thank you for my Shield of Faith, for my sword, and for the victory that you have given me today.*" Upon release, the parchment shot from his hand.

He stood to his feet and placed the book reverently inside his doublet, close to his heart. A song of joy and gratitude burst from his lips as he resumed his journey. He had met the enemy face to face and experienced the sweet taste of victory!

Two or three furlongs further down the path he heard the rustling in the darkness of the forest again, but this time it didn't frighten him. He didn't even bother to draw his sword. He laughed softly. The enemy knew better than to tangle with him.

"Let him that thinketh he standeth take heed lest he fall," a quiet voice whispered, but Josiah didn't hear. He marched along resolutely.

Hearing a noise in the branches of a huge tree that overhung the trail, Josiah looked up just in time to see a dark figure dropping straight at him. He tried to dodge, but he was too late. A heavy body struck him full in the shoulder, knocking him face down to the earth.

Josiah reached for his sword, but a strong hand gripped his wrist and a sharp blade pressed menacingly against the side of his neck. He froze, afraid to move. Rough hands jerked him to his feet. A hand of steel reached inside his doublet, and then was quickly snatched back out.

Laughter rang through the darkness of the forest as strong hands hurled Josiah headlong into a patch of briars at the side of the trail. He rolled free of the briars and leaped to his feet. The forest was dark and silent; he was alone on the trail. His attackers had disappeared as quickly as they had come.

Thoroughly frightened, the young prince reached for his book. His heart seemed to skip a beat as he realized that the weapon was not there. His assailants had stolen his sword! He was helpless!

A slight noise caught his attention and he looked upward to see the dove perched in the branches of a shagbark hickory. "They came back," Josiah lamented. "I had a complete victory over them, and yet they came back and attacked me a second time! They took my sword."

"He who experiences victory often leaves himself open to a second attack," the dove replied quietly.

"Aye, but I beat them so easily the first time!" Josiah exclaimed. "I didn't think they'd come back!" He looked accusingly at the celestial bird. "Why didn't you warn me?"

"I tried," the dove rejoined, "but you weren't listening. Your heart was too full of your victory to hear my admonitions and warnings."

Josiah hung his head. "I never dreamed that they would come back like that," he lamented. "The first victory was so easy." He sighed deeply. "And now I've lost my sword."

"Sometimes a warrior is most vulnerable just after he has won his greatest victory. Ecstatic with success, he lets his guard down, and immediately the enemy moves in to take advantage of his carelessness."

The young prince nodded sadly. "Aye, that is what has happened to me, I fear. The first victory was so easy that I neglected to watch for the enemy. Were those Argamor's men?"

"Indeed they were."

"Woe is me, for I am in desperate trouble," Josiah lamented. "I am unarmed, and the enemy knows where I am. What shall I do?"

"First and foremost, you must get your sword back," the dove replied. "You are lost without it." He spread his snowy wings. "Follow me, my prince. I will lead you to a place of safety until it is time for you to make your assault on the enemy."

The young prince gasped. "Assault? I am to attack? But I have no sword!"

"And that is precisely why you must face the enemy. You must retrieve your sword, or you shall never reach the Castle of Knowledge." The dove took to the air and Josiah hurried after him.

Josiah crouched behind the roots of an ancient oak, watching in silence as the band of dark knights talked and jested and laughed around a crackling campfire. The flames leaped high, creating mysterious dancing shadows that seemed to leap and prance about on the trunks of the trees surrounding the enemy camp. The young prince noted with delight that none of the men now wore armor or weapons; those items had been carelessly discarded in a disorderly heap at the base of a huge, gnarled sycamore. He also noted with an equal amount of delight that many of the men were staring into the fire, watching the bright figures that seemed to spring from the wood to leap and dance and disappear within the glowing caverns of the flames. Sir Faithful had taught him that a man who stares into a campfire ruins his night vision momentarily, rendering himself helpless against a surprise attack in the dark. The enemy knights were letting down their guard!

The tallest of the dark knights, a fierce-looking man with snapping black eyes, a thick, black beard, and a hideous battle scar across his right cheek, drew a sword and swung it about. Josiah choked back an exclamation of surprise when he saw that the glittering weapon was his own. The dark knight had *his sword*!

The tall knight stepped close to the fire and held the weapon over the flames, examining it in the flickering firelight. The other knights crowded closer, seemingly interested in the sword. "Quite a blade, Lord Dubious," one said.

The tall knight laughed. "Aye, but the young prince possesses it no longer. He is now helpless as a newborn lamb." Laughter greeted his words.

"Why did we not run the prince through when we had him in our power?" another complained. "We should never have let him go!"

Lord Dubious, obviously the leader of the band, shook his head. "Nay. Our orders were to disarm the young prince, not kill him. Lord Argamor was quite firm on that score."

"I still say we should have done him in."

"Fool!" Lord Dubious was clearly losing patience. "Do you not know who the young prince is? He is the son—" the knight gulped and then continued, "of King Emmanuel! We could not have killed him if we had tried. Lord Argamor himself could not have killed him. We can only do what the King allows, no more."

Another knight snorted in derision. "Aye, so the mighty Lord Argamor is subservient to King Emmanuel? Methinks that perhaps we are serving the wrong master."

The tall knight seized the speaker by the throat and shook him furiously. "Hold your tongue!" he raged. "If your words fall upon Lord Argamor's ears, we are all dead men!" Releasing his fellow knight, Lord Dubious backed away from the fire until he was standing less than twelve feet from Josiah's hiding place. "All of you hold your tongues!" he declared vehemently, stabbing the air with Josiah's sword for emphasis.

"When Dubious turns around, seize the sword and charge Argamor's knights," a still, small voice instructed Josiah. "Do not hesitate; the victory will be yours."

Josiah tensed. *One unarmed youth against thirteen enemy knights? What chance of success could I possibly have?* Fear overwhelmed him, and he began to tremble uncontrollably. If he went unarmed against Lord Dubious' band of knights he could not possibly hope for victory—they would tear him to pieces.

But then he remembered the words of Sir Faithful. Speaking of the dove, the elderly steward of the Castle of Faith had told Josiah, "Learn to listen for his voice, for he will never lead you wrong. Obedience to his voice will guarantee success in your journey to the seven castles." Josiah took a deep breath. *If Sir Faithful was right, then I need to trust and obey the dove, even though I can see no way to win victory over thirteen of Argamor's knights.* He took another deep breath. The decision was made. *Aye, I'll do it!*

Dubious turned at that moment, and the firelight flashed golden upon the glittering blade of Josiah's sword. To Josiah's surprise, the tall knight was playing with the weapon, balancing it vertically in the palm of his hand with the hilt uppermost and the point of the blade pressing into his flesh.

Josiah sprang from the shadows with the speed of a panther, snatched the powerful sword from the grasp of the startled knight, and swung the glittering weapon with all his might. With a shout of triumph he leaped toward the fire, charging straight at the group of wide-eyed knights who jumped to their feet and scattered into the darkness like a flock of game birds. Encouraged by his success, the young prince swung about to face Dubious.

The tall leader of the band of knights dashed across the clearing and snatched up a sword from the base of the sycamore. He lifted the weapon overhead with both hands, whirled about, and charged straight at Josiah. With a snarl of rage he brought the sword down viciously.

Josiah met steel with steel. The blade of his sword repelled that of his attacker with a loud clang that rang through the forest.

Dubious raised his sword again. "You shall die tonight, knave!" he screamed in fury. "Forget Argamor's orders—I shall run you through!" Grunting with the effort, he swung his deadly sword with all his strength. The blade flashed through the air in a glittering arc that was intended to take off Josiah's head.

But Josiah was no longer on the defensive. He leaped forward, swinging his own sword in a lightning-quick movement that Sir Faithful had taught him. The invincible weapon cut cleanly through the blade of his tall adversary, penetrated the dark knight's armor, and inflicted a mortal wound.

Howling with pain and anger, Dubious whirled about and vanished into the night. Just as the dove had said, Josiah had experienced a complete victory.

With the flutter of snowy wings, the dove flew down and alighted in the top of a five-foot sapling. "They're gone!" Josiah exulted. "My sword has completely vanquished the enemy."

"They have prepared you a fire," the dove told him. "Take your rest until the dawn of the morning light."

"Here?" Josiah was aghast. "But what if they return?"

"They will not return tonight."

"But I don't know that for sure!" Josiah protested. "How can I sleep, knowing that Dubious and his knights might return at any moment and take me captive?"

"Do you trust me?" the dove asked, cocking his head to one side and regarding him with unblinking eyes.

"Well, aye, but..."

"Then leave your safety in my care and take your rest. I will watch over you tonight. Dubious and his men shall not return to harm you. When you lie down, you shall not be afraid: yea, you shall lie down, and your sleep shall be sweet."

Reassured by the words of his gentle guide, Josiah lay down beside the fire, wrapped his cloak about his head, and fell asleep almost instantly.

Chapter Eight

The morning sun cast brilliant ruby rays across the dewy, fog-shrouded forest as Prince Josiah trudged down the winding trail. Refreshed by a good night's sleep and a breakfast of bread, cheese and wild berries, the young prince was anxious to resume his journey to the Castle of Knowledge. He took the time to cut a sturdy walking staff, knowing that he had a long day's journey ahead of him.

The trail wound its way out of the shadowy forest, widened, and merged with a sun-splashed, well traveled road that stretched ahead as far as the eye could see. Small farms appeared on both sides of the roadway as he hiked along. Tiny green shoots were just beginning to poke their heads through the deep brown earth of the freshly plowed fields; clusters of snowy white blackberry blossoms graced the humble wooden fences bordering the lane. Tall, stately maples along the road were bedecked with new buds. The air was filled with the fragrance of wild flowers and the steady hum of the many bees diligently attending to them. The land of Terrestria was celebrating the freshness of spring.

Hearing the squeak of a carriage overtaking him, Josiah moved to the side of the road to allow it to pass. A sleek black hansom pulled by a single gray horse swept by, slowed, and then rolled to a stop just yards ahead of him. "Would you care to ride, my lord?" a friendly voice called.

Josiah hurried to the side of the vehicle and looked up to see a thin-faced man seated within the carriage. He could tell immediately by the traveler's bearing and the cut of his clothing that the man was well educated. "Aye, sire, if it pleases you," Josiah replied politely.

"It pleases me well, my lord," the hansom driver said with a cheerful grin. "Welcome aboard!"

Seconds later the carriage rolled forward with Josiah seated comfortably on a plush seat of scarlet velvet. He leaned back against the seat and relaxed. "I thank you, sire."

"Aye, it is my privilege to carry a prince such as yourself," the man replied. "My name is Skeptic. And where might you be traveling today?"

"I am Prince Josiah, of the Castle of Faith. I'm on my way to the Castle of Knowledge."

"The Castle of Knowledge? And what business would you have there, my lord?"

"I'm on a quest for King Emmanuel, and I am traveling to the Castle of Knowledge as a learning experience."

"One can never obtain enough knowledge," Skeptic said, nodding agreeably. "I spent a number of years at Cowford University myself and managed to acquire more than one sheepskin. Aye, indeed, knowledge is a valuable thing." He threw a sideways glance at Josiah. "And what field of study will you engage yourself in at the Castle of Knowledge?"

"I will study the book, sire."

"The book? My lord, there are many books. Of which book do you speak?"

Josiah reached inside his doublet and pulled out his precious volume. "The book," he repeated. "King Emmanuel's book. I am traveling to the Castle of Knowledge so that I may learn more of the truth of the book, and of King Emmanuel."

Skeptic chuckled. "You have made use of the word 'truth'. You do realize, of course, that truth is relative?"

"What do you mean, sire?"

The man glanced at the book with a look of disdain. "Truth is truth only when it is perceived as truth in the mind of the one seeking truth," he said, giving the reins a flick and urging the horse to a gentle trot. "What is truth for one person may not of necessity be entirely truth for another, and may be completely untruth for yet a third."

Josiah frowned. "I don't understand, sire. Truth is truth, and always will be." He lifted the book with both hands. "I know that this is truth, for it came from King Emmanuel."

"It may be truth for you," Skeptic answered suavely, "but perhaps it is not truth for the next fellow."

"If it's truth, then it's true for everyone!" Josiah retorted.

His companion shook his head. "Not necessarily. Let me illustrate what I mean, my lord. Have you ever eaten veal basted in almond sauce?"

Josiah nodded. "Aye."

"Would you agree with the statement that veal basted in almond sauce is the finest dish ever served to man?"

Josiah shook his head. "Nay, not really. There are many dishes that I like much better."

Skeptic smiled. "Then you will understand what I am saying. From where I sit, veal basted in almond sauce is the finest food available in all Terrestria; there is no finer. And yet for you, there are others foods that you would rather eat. So what is truth for me—namely, that veal in almond sauce is the finest food—is not necessarily truth to you." He turned and faced

Josiah. "Do you understand, my lord?"

"Aye," Josiah said slowly, "but—" Skeptic's words made sense in a way, and yet, down in his heart, he knew that something was wrong with the man's logic.

"It's the same with your book," the man continued. "Parts of it may be truth to you and other parts truth to me; but the parts that are truth to you may not be truth to me and the parts that are truth to me may not be truth to you; and certainly not all of it is truth to both you and me."

"But all of it is truth!" Josiah protested. "It was given to me by King Emmanuel!"

"Aye, but King Emmanuel did not actually write it," Skeptic said smoothly.

Josiah was shocked. "Then who did?" he challenged.

"King Emmanuel commissioned various men to write the various parts. It was a huge project that took many years. I'm sure that the writers were good men and meant well, but as I was saying, what is truth for one is not always truth for another. Your book contains truth, to be sure, but not all of it is truth. And certainly not all of it is truth for every man, not even you."

He laid a hand on Josiah's knee in a friendly gesture. "Prince Josiah, I am a man of learning. I spent a number of my years in diligent study at Cowford, yet in all my learning I discovered that it is necessary to determine for oneself what is truth for oneself, and what is to be rejected. And I have also discovered that what was truth yesterday may not necessarily be truth today."

Josiah and Skeptic continued to argue and discuss the matter as the hansom rolled smoothly along. The man's arguments were based on half-truths, yet they contained just enough of the element of truth to sound convincing, and that was what confused Josiah. The young prince listened to the smooth words of the intelligent, highly educated man and he began to wonder. *What if Skeptic is right? Is truth relative? If a certain truth is truth to me, does it really have to be truth for everyone else?* A troubling thought came to mind just then. *What if certain parts of King Emmanuel's book are not truth for me? And how will I know which parts are truth and which are not?*

"I must leave you here," Skeptic said, interrupting Josiah's thoughts and snapping him back to the reality of the present. The hansom had come to a stop at a fork in the road. "My travels take me down this lane to the left, but if you are traveling to the Castle of Knowledge you will want the road to the right. Have a pleasant journey, Prince Josiah."

Josiah scrambled down from the comfortable carriage, slightly disappointed at the prospect of having to walk again. "I thank you, sire. I enjoyed the ride."

"Aye, young prince, and I thank you. I enjoyed your company." With a flick of the whip and a shake of the reins, Skeptic set the horse to pulling the hansom at a brisk pace down the road to the left.

Josiah stared at his surroundings in astonishment and dismay. During the ride in the comfortable carriage, his attention had been so focused on Skeptic's words that he had paid no attention to the passing scenery. Now he found himself standing in the middle of a sandy track that led across a wind-blown desert. There was not a single green tree or flower or patch of grass for as far as the eye could see, just miles and miles of barren, red-brown rock and dull sand that stretched all the way to the horizon. Stunned, Josiah turned around, but the view was the same behind him.

Spotting a single tree in the distance beside the road, he hurried toward it. But when he reached it he discovered nothing but the lifeless skeleton of a tree that had perished long before. A hideous vulture with a great, ugly neck and drooping, oily feathers perched high in one of the dead branches. Josiah shuddered.

The young prince did not know it, but Skeptic had taken him into the Desert of Doubt, a vast, arid wasteland of skepticism and unbelief. It was a perilous place of treacherous winds, shifting sands and ravenous predators that had claimed the life of many a pilgrim before him. The roadway upon which he stood stretched across the barren landscape in a straight line to disappear over the crest of a bare hillock of sun-baked earth. A large, blood red scorpion scurried across the trail and darted into the shade of a large rock, holding his venomous stinger poised for action.

Josiah stared with a growing sense of dread at the empty wasteland stretching before him. Death and decay seemed to be staring right back at him. He shuddered as a cold, lonely chill swept over him. Never before had he felt so alone, so tiny, and so vulnerable. He sighed. "How will I ever cross this?" he asked aloud, startling himself with the sound of his own voice. "I have no food, no water, and there doesn't appear to be any for miles and miles. What if I am not even heading in the right direction?"

He drew the book from his bosom and opened it to seek direction. A nagging doubt played in his mind. What if the book was not always true? What if it was true only some of the time, or if only some parts were true and others were not? How would he know the difference? What if the book was to lead him astray, if but only once? What if this was that one time?

Unsettled by Skeptic's arguments and unsure now of the trustworthiness of his beloved book, he sadly closed its pages and slipped it reluctantly into his doublet. He had depended so many times upon the book for guidance, and now felt a tremendous sense of loss. If the book was not *always* true then he simply could not trust it.

An even more disturbing thought entered his troubled mind. The book had been given to him by King Emmanuel; but so had his Parchment of Assurance. If the book could not be trusted, what about his parchment—the precious document that declared him to be the son of King Emmanuel forever? Josiah was in anguish as he thought about it.

He sighed and started forward, stabbing irritably at the powdery sand with the tip of his walking staff. The wind howled and moaned like a vengeful banshee, throwing sand and dust in his face as if it resented his presence. Within moments his eyes were stinging and his mouth felt parched and hot. The dismal Desert of Doubt seemed to be drawing the very life from his body and soul.

Hours later Josiah stumbled wearily to the top of a gentle slope and paused to survey the dreary, colorless landscape before him. The walking staff was gone, but he was not even aware of the loss. His throat was parched; his tongue was swollen; his lips were cracked and bleeding. The blazing white sun seemed to be ten times its usual size; his eyes burned from the intense glare. The merciless wind shrieked in fury as it hurled handfuls of blinding sand into his face. Shielding his eyes and mouth against the fiery sun and the relentless wind, he staggered down the slope and dropped to the ground behind an outcropping of red sandstone. He had to get out of this sun and wind.

He rubbed his stinging eyes, but the grit on his hands merely made matters worse. *Water! I have to have water!* Panting like a dog, he rested in the shade of the rocky ledge. *If I stay here, I'll die. But I simply can't continue much further like this.* With a sigh of resignation, he pulled himself to his feet.

His heart leaped. Less than a furlong away, a small pond sparkled beside the roadway! Cool and blue and inviting, the water glittered in the blazing sun like a king's ransom of jewels. His steps quickened with new energy as he hurried toward it. Water! He could now see the distant mountains reflected in the shimmering surface.

Delirious with joy, Josiah knelt at the pond's edge and thrust in his hands to dip up a double handful of the precious, life-giving liquid. But his fingers came up with sand and dust; the pond had disappeared. Stunned, he stared at the barren ground, which seemed to mock him with its stark reality. Just moments before there had been a shimmering pond of water; now there was only sand and dust. He staggered to his feet.

Less than a hundred paces away lay another pond. He stared long and hard, afraid that this oasis too would disappear. The water was real—he could see the ripples caused by the wind. He tottered in that direction. Suddenly he felt like screaming. The second pond had also vanished like an ethereal wisp of his imagination. "But the water was real," he sobbed. "I saw it!"

Spotting another body of water nearby, Josiah hobbled desperately toward it. He slowly became aware of a heavy weight that thumped repeatedly against his aching body, so he reached inside his doublet. His trembling fingers pulled out the cumbersome object and he stared at it as though he had never seen it before. The book! Somehow he had never before realized just how heavy the volume really was. He lowered his hand to drop the book into the sand.

"Nay!" a voice within him seemed to cry. "The book was given you by King Emmanuel!" His hand seemed to move of its own accord as he again placed the sacred book within the folds of his doublet. He stumbled forward, heedless of the deadly desert viper coiled beside the trail.

The weary young prince wandered hopelessly from one mirage to another, gradually growing weaker and weaker. Each time, the water seemed so real and so close that he had to try to reach it. But each and every time the imagined oasis would vanish before he could quite get to it. Thoroughly spent and unable to go further, Josiah sank to his knees in the middle of the lonely road. The sun beat down relentlessly. High overhead, three dark vultures circled in anticipation. The Desert of Doubt was preparing to claim another victim.

Chapter Nine

Prince Josiah lay senseless upon the burning sands of the Desert of Doubt, thoroughly spent and defeated. Skeptic's persuasive arguments had confused and bewildered him. The man's unbelief was like a contagious disease, sapping the strength and life from Josiah's trusting soul.

He longed for water. The sun was so unrelenting, the wind so dry and the sands so hot. Unaware of the fact that he was dehydrating and could not survive long, he simply longed for a cool drink to soothe his parched throat. He moaned aloud. His head dropped listlessly, and though the sand burned his cheek, he did not move.

Gradually he realized that the blazing sun did not seem as brilliant as it had been. Summoning his strength, he slowly lifted his head. Somehow he found himself lying in the shade of a tall spire of red rock. *Impossible*, he thought, *I didn't have the strength to move.* His eyes fell closed.

Josiah slowly became aware of a gentle hand caressing his burning brow. The touch was cool and comforting. He opened his eyes. He was on his back, staring up into the face of a beautiful young woman with long, raven black hair. She was arrayed in a long, flowing robe so white that it was dazzling to look at.

One of the bright ones! I must be seeing one of the bright ones! Am I in the Golden City of the Redeemed?

"Prince Josiah, of the Castle of Faith," a soft voice said, "I have been sent to help you in your time of trouble." The voice was gentle, soothing, like the musical tones of a harp.

"Who are you?" Josiah asked, attempting to raise his head for another glimpse of the lovely ethereal personage. His tongue was thick and swollen, and he had trouble speaking. He found it difficult to keep his eyes open.

"My name is Faith," the musical voice replied. The gentle fingers stroked his forehead again, cool and soothing. "I live with my sisters Hope and Charity in the region just beyond the mountains. This dreadful wasteland in which we are now is the Desert of Doubt."

"How did I get here in the shade?" Josiah asked. "Did you move me?"

"You are still where you have fallen," the woman replied. "I moved the column of rock to shade you."

Josiah's eyes flew open. "That's impossible!"

Her laughter was like the tinkle of a silver bell. "I can move mountains, Prince Josiah."

"Am I to die here, my lady?"

"King Emmanuel sent me to you," Faith said softly. "Prince Josiah, arise and drink." She helped him to a sitting position.

He looked around. "But I see no water."

"You have it with you," she answered. "The water of life is found within your book."

Josiah reached into his doublet with a trembling hand and slowly withdrew the book. "Open it up," Faith directed.

As Prince Josiah opened the pages of his book, a stream of water poured from within, cool and clear and pure. Josiah stared for a moment, and then began to drink ravenously. The water seemed sweeter than any other he had ever tasted. He drank deeply, enjoying the refreshing coolness. He drank until he thought he could hold no more.

"Drink again," Faith said.

"But I have had enough, my lady. I am fully satisfied."

"Drink again." The look in her eyes told him that it was useless to argue, and so he simply obeyed. Again, the water was sweet and cool and refreshing.

When he stopped, she smiled. "Drink again."

He did, and felt new life and energy surge through his soul. Finally, he closed the book, but Faith did not protest. He wiped his mouth with the back of his hand, surprised to see that his skin was fresh and clean. "I really thought that I was going to die. I saw the vultures circling overhead."

"The Desert of Doubt has claimed the life of many a pilgrim, my prince. One cannot survive long without the water that flows from the book."

Josiah dropped his eyes, suddenly feeling humbled and unworthy. "I don't know how I even came here, Faith. A man named 'Skeptic' offered me a ride in his carriage, and the next thing I knew, I was in this wretched desert."

"Unbelief is a deadly foe, Prince Josiah," Faith said softly. Her voice was quiet and gentle; her eyes were filled with understanding and concern. Josiah searched her face for some indication of condemnation, but there was not a trace. "A man like Skeptic spreads his unbelief like a plague, and there is no antidote for unbelief except faith. Faith is a gift from King Emmanuel that comes through his book."

She stood to her feet. "Are you strong enough to continue your journey?"

Josiah was already experiencing the rejuvenating effects of the life-giving water. "I am ready," he said. He stood, and Faith began to lead him down the dusty road. Somehow the sun did not seem so large nor its heat so intense. He was stronger, and he knew it.

"Skeptic told me that truth is not always truth," the young prince reported, striding briskly along beside his lovely companion. "It was very confusing, but I think what he said was that what is truth for one person may not be truth for another. Or something such as that. Anyway, he said that my book is not always truth and certainly not truth for every person."

"Truth is truth," Faith told him, "regardless of whether or not one believes. Your book came from King Emmanuel, so we know that it is truth. And truth is for all."

"Aye, my lady, that's what I tried to tell him. But he twisted my words so easily, and his arguments seemed so convincing. He had me so confused that I was ready to quit believing the Word of my King!"

Faith smiled. "Skeptic is an emissary for Argamor. And remember, Argamor is the master of lies and double-talk."

"Skeptic told me that truth for one person may not be truth for another person. For instance, he said that he believes that veal is the finest food available, but I might not believe that veal is the best, so that might not be truth for me. In a way, that made sense, and in a way it didn't. Do you know what I mean?"

"Skeptic is deliberately confusing *truth* with *opinion* in order to confuse you and lead you astray. Do you know the difference between *truth* and *opinion*?"

"What do you mean, my lady?"

"Suppose that I tell you that veal is a food. We both know that statement to be *truth*—veal *is* a food. Whether you agree with that statement or not changes nothing. But suppose I tell you that veal is the finest food in all Terrestria—that statement would simply be my *opinion*. Do you see the difference?"

Josiah nodded.

"Truth never changes, Prince Josiah. Even if every last soul in Terrestria refuses to believe the truth of your book, it is still truth. Opinions may change and vary from person to person, but truth never does."

Josiah and Faith followed the road as it descended a gentle slope. Josiah stopped and stared in utter amazement. "Oh, my!"

Before them lay a quiet valley, bright with life and promise. To the right of the road was a thriving apple orchard with branches so laden with blossoms that the trees appeared to be covered with snow. Wildflowers grew in colorful abundance to the left of the road; their fragrance seemed to Josiah the very essence of life. A crystal-clear brook laughed merrily as it crossed the roadway beneath a stone bridge and then meandered through acres and acres of brilliant blue flowers. Thousands of yellow butterflies danced in the air. In the very center of the beautiful valley stood a castle of the purest white stone.

A rainbow with seven colors hung over the valley, bold and brilliant against the deep blue of the cloudless sky. "It's the rainbow of promise!" Josiah breathed. He looked in bewilderment at Faith. "What happened to the Desert of Doubt? It seemed that we had furlongs and furlongs and furlongs still to go, but all of a sudden, the desert just disappeared!"

Faith smiled. "You chose to believe your King, Prince Josiah. The Desert of Doubt cannot exist when your faith is strong." She pointed to the castle in the valley. "Behold the Castle of Knowledge, my prince. A welcome awaits you."

With joy in his heart the young prince studied the Castle of Knowledge. "The rainbow is directly above the castle!" he said, turning to Faith. "It's as if the—" He stopped, openmouthed, and stared at the spot where Faith had stood just moments before. His lovely companion had vanished.

Josiah hurried down the slope toward the Castle of Knowledge. His heart was light; the horrible experience of the Desert of Doubt was behind him and he looked forward with eager anticipation to his visit at the castle.

"If it's knowledge you are after, my lord, perhaps I can help," a friendly female voice called, and Josiah looked over to see a heavyset woman with a jolly countenance standing by a tree beside the road. The tree was surrounded by a three-foot wrought iron fence, and so heavily laden with luscious-looking fruit that its branches nearly touched the ground. "This is the tree of the knowledge of good and evil, my lord," the woman told him, plucking one of the fruit and polishing it with the sleeve of her gown. "Its fruit is greatly desired, for it can make one wise."

Prince Josiah approached the magnificent tree. "Wisdom and knowledge are what I seek, my lady," he said politely.

The woman held the fruit out to Josiah. As he reached for it, his eye fell upon a small sign upon the fence, which said, ***"NO TRESPASSING. By the royal decree of King Emmanuel."***

Josiah quickly stepped back. "Nay, my lady," he said decisively. "This tree and its fruit are forbidden. The sign says so."

The temptress laughed. "Your King will never know," she countered slyly, "and the fruit *is* a source of knowledge and wisdom."

"Never!" Josiah declared. "I will not disobey my King!" With these words he turned his back on the woman and strode purposefully toward the castle.

As he approached the main gate, the young prince was amazed to see that the Castle of Knowledge was tiny, by far the smallest castle he had seen yet. *This castle would fit within the Castle of Faith a dozen times with space left over,* he told himself. *This castle is so small!*

The drawbridge was down and the portcullis was up, so Josiah stepped boldly onto the drawbridge to be met by a knight in white armor. "Identify yourself, my lord," the knight requested pleasantly.

"I am Prince Josiah of the Castle of Faith, royal heir to King Emmanuel."

"What is your business at the Castle of Knowledge?"

"I have been sent by King Emmanuel," Josiah replied.

The guard stepped to one side. "Enter, my lord, and may your stay at the castle be a pleasant one."

A young man of slender build hurried forward to greet Josiah, adjusting his spectacles and flashing a friendly smile as he entered the gatehouse. "Welcome to the Castle of Knowledge, my young friend! You must be Prince Josiah."

"Indeed I am," Josiah replied. "I have been sent by King Emmanuel."

"Aye, we have been expecting you," the enthusiastic man told him. "My name is Student, and I am delighted that you are here." Behind the round lenses of his spectacles, Student's eyes sparkled with an intensity that told Josiah that his host meant every word. "I am the castle steward, and my purpose is to assist you in obtaining a deeper, fuller knowledge of your King." His eyes seemed to glow as he said, "The more that one learns of His Majesty, the more one loves him."

Josiah nodded, encouraged by Student's exuberant welcome. "I love my King with all my heart, and I am anxious to learn more of him that I may serve him better."

Together the prince and the castle steward strolled through a tiny courtyard alive with flowering trees and colorful flower gardens. A small spring bubbled up in the center of the courtyard; the crystal-clear water flowed along a rock-lined channel and disappeared beneath the wall at the opposite end. "Your solar will be in the east tower," Student said, pointing toward the upper corner of the castle wall, "but first I will take you to the Library of Learning."

Josiah followed him through a doorway and then paused in utter amazement. He and the castle steward were standing on the polished marble floor of a room so immense that Josiah could not see the far end. There was no furniture in the vast room; but the walls were adorned with enormous, gilt-framed paintings that reached from floor to ceiling. Josiah shook his head in bewilderment. The library appeared to be twenty times larger than the entire Castle of Knowledge! How could such a huge library fit within such a tiny castle?

"This is the Library of Learning, the most important chamber in the Castle of Knowledge," his host was saying. "You are welcome to visit this room as often as you would wish, and to stay as long as you would wish."

"But there are no books!" Josiah protested. "Why is this room called the 'Library of Learning'?"

"Oh, my prince, but there are books," Student corrected gently. "Sixty-six volumes, to be exact." He gestured toward the nearest wall. "The paintings that you see are in reality volumes of wisdom and instruction. Some give the history of Terrestria; others simply relate or explain His Majesty's edicts and commandments." He stepped closer to a huge picture that depicted a beautiful outdoor scene with purple mountains, a flowing river and a luscious garden. As Josiah moved toward the painting, he was amazed to see that the scene was alive with movement—the river in the picture was actually flowing; the leaves on the trees fluttered in a gentle breeze; birds flew from branch to branch. The effect was that of looking through a window.

"This is the Book of Beginnings," Student told the astonished young prince. "One may enter it to learn the story of how King Emmanuel created Terrestria, and how Argamor enticed the first residents into a foolish rebellion against their King."

"*Enter* the volume, my lord?" Josiah repeated. "How would one enter the volume?"

"Simply step into the picture and you will go back into another dimension of time," Student replied, "in order to visit the lands and the people described in your book and witness for yourself the events described therein. Once you are inside, the inhabitants of the land cannot see you, nor will they be aware of your presence. But you will see and hear everything in order that you may learn more about King Emmanuel and his plans for Terrestria."

"Amazing!" Josiah said softly. "I've never seen anything like this!"

Student shrugged. "That is precisely what happens every time that you open your book to read," he pointed out. "The Library of Learning simply brings the same information to life."

An exciting thought suddenly occurred to Josiah, and he turned eagerly to Student. "My book tells of King Emmanuel and his life here in Terrestria. Would any of these volumes show me those events?"

"Follow me," Student told him. "There are four volumes that record His Majesty's life here upon Terrestria, and you may explore them to your heart's content. They're in the New

Wing of the library." The footsteps of the steward and the prince echoed throughout the vast chamber as they walked across the Library of Learning.

"The library is divided into two main wings, which we still call the Old and the New," the castle steward explained. "The Old Wing contains thirty-nine volumes, and was completed long before King Emmanuel returned for his visit to Terrestria. Four hundred years after the Old Wing was completed, His Majesty had some major remodeling done and then started construction on the New Wing. It contains twenty-seven volumes."

Josiah's eyes were wide as he followed his host across the vast marble floor. "The first five volumes in the Old Wing," Student said, gesturing toward the first group of giant pictures, "are known as the books of the Law. They record the beginning of Terrestria, the rebellion of the inhabitants, and King Emmanuel's laws governing his subjects. Then come the books of History, which are exactly what the name implies. There's a section of Poetry, all of which was written to praise our King, and then a section of Prophecy."

"What is prophecy?" Josiah asked.

"In the prophecy section, King Emmanuel reveals his plans for Terrestria. One can actually learn much of what is going to happen in the future by visiting in those volumes."

After passing a number of the enormous paintings, Josiah and Student stepped through a doorway covered by a thick veil and entered a second room nearly as large as the first. The steward paused before the first picture. "These four volumes are the ones for which you are looking," he told Josiah. "By entering any one of these, you may observe the life of your King while he was here in Terrestria."

"How may I get back out of the volume, sire?"

"Oh," Student replied, with a sheepish grin, "I suppose I forgot to tell you. Enter the volume with your book open to the story that you would like to visit. When you are ready to leave, simply close your book and you will find yourself back within the Library of Learning." He laid a hand on Josiah's arm. "But remember, Prince Josiah, the inhabitants of the time that you are about to visit cannot see or hear you, nor will they be aware of your presence. You cannot talk to them, nor will they speak to you. You are merely an observer."

Josiah stepped to the base of the first enormous picture. He drew the precious book from within his doublet and opened it to a particular page. A thrill of excitement swept over him as he lifted his foot to step over the frame of the picture and into the volume.

Chapter Ten

Prince Josiah took a deep breath and stepped into the giant picture. In the next instant he found himself standing in the center of an enormous crowd of noisy, excited people. Looking about, he realized that they were in the courtyard of a large, magnificent building. The throng of people around him seemed to be waiting for some momentous event to take place; they pushed and shoved and chattered excitedly as they fought for good viewing places.

Right beside Josiah was a large, sturdily built woman wearing the garments of a simple peasant. Her face was radiant as she waited expectantly. In her eagerness to see, she crowded against Josiah until she was almost on top of him. "Excuse me, my good woman," Josiah protested, "but would you be so kind as to allow me a little more room? You are nearly standing on my foot!"

But the heavy woman acted as if she had not heard. Totally ignoring Josiah, she crowded closer and closer until her large sandaled foot was actually on top of Josiah's. To Josiah's surprise, he felt no pain—not even the sensation of weight on his foot. Looking down, the young prince was astonished to see that the woman's foot occupied the same space as his own—her foot seemed to pass right through his. Puzzled, he stepped away from her.

A young boy darted through the crowd, dodging left and right as he pushed his way through the throng of excited people. He headed right for Josiah. As the peasant boy ran at him, Josiah raised his hands to protect himself. To his utter astonishment, there was no collision. The lad ran right through him!

Josiah stared in amazement, and then he remembered Student's words: "Remember, Josiah, that the inhabitants of the time that you are about to visit cannot see or hear you, nor will they be aware of your presence." *So I don't really exist in this place,* Josiah told himself. *I can see and hear these people, but they can't hear or see me, because I am not really here. I can occupy the same space and pass right through them because in reality, I am in another dimension of time.* He didn't quite understand his own explanation, but to him it made sense.

To test his theory, the young prince walked straight toward a tight cluster of people. To his delight, his body passed right through the mass of humanity without encountering any obstacles whatever. He stopped beside a small family—a cheerful young mother holding a girl by the hand and a tall, thin father with a small boy on his shoulders.

"Father, will I be able to see the King?" the boy called eagerly.

"I hope so, my son," the man replied. "They say that he is to pass right by us on his way to the palace."

"Will he talk to me, Father?" The boy's eyes were bright with excitement.

The young mother laughed. "Kings don't have time for children, my son," she said gently. "Kings are always busy with more important matters."

"They don't talk to peasants anyway, Timothy," the father

spoke up. "We need to content ourselves with the mere sight of His Majesty as his coach passes."

"But *I* won't get to see him," a small voice whined, and Josiah glanced down at the skinny girl who clutched her mother's hand so tightly. "Timothy will get to see the King, but I won't get to see anybody! Can't you hold me up, too?"

"I'll hold Timothy up until he sees the King," her father promised, "and then I'll try to hold you up, too, Miriam."

"Father, why is King Emmanuel coming to our city?" Timothy asked, leaning down in an attempt to see his father's face. "Is he going to live here now?"

"He's coming to meet with some very important men," the humble peasant answered. "It will just be a short visit."

"I wish he could stay here forever so we could see him and talk with him and play with him," Miriam said wistfully. "They say that our King is the kindest king who ever lived!"

"He's coming! His Majesty the King is coming!" The cry swept across the crowd of peasants and they surged forward, eager for a glimpse of the royal visitor. They tramped right across the space that Josiah occupied, passing right through him. Uncomfortable at the sensation of having strangers walk through him, Josiah stepped to one side.

A regal white coach resplendent with golden fittings rolled down the avenue and entered the courtyard. Above the glistening coach flew a royal purple standard emblazoned with the emblems of a cross and a golden crown. The crowd parted to make way for the imperial vehicle and its four prancing white horses, and the coach came to a stop just yards from where Josiah stood.

Behind the coach, a cavalcade of knights in shining armor sat astride snowy white chargers. The royal purple banner flying grandly from the tip of each man's lance carried the same cross and crown emblem as the coach. As Josiah watched, the knights dismounted and stood at attention beside their magnificent horses. The spirited chargers pranced and pawed the earth. Awed by the majesty of the moment, the people fell silent.

Golden trumpets sounded a royal fanfare as the coach door opened and the King stepped out. The people fell to their knees to show their respect for their royal visitor. Several important and stately dignitaries stepped forward to greet the King. A hush fell over the crowd as the King and his entourage moved slowly away from the royal coach and went to meet the waiting group of important leaders.

At that moment a young boy dashed through the crowd, slipped past the guards surrounding the regal assemblage, and approached King Emmanuel himself. "King, I'm glad that you're here!" the little boy cried, extending his small hand and grasping the strong hand of the King. "Thank you for coming to visit us!" A gasp of astonishment and fear swept across the crowd. How would the royal visitor respond to such brashness?

Josiah was surprised to realize that the eager little boy was Timothy, the lad who just moments before had been perched on his father's shoulders.

Two burly guards seized the boy by the arms, jerking him upward and backward as they hurried him away from King Emmanuel. "Away with you, lad!" one cried. "No one approaches His Majesty in such a manner! He has no time for peasant children such as yourself!" The look of awe on the lad's face was instantly replaced by a look of terror.

"Guards!" The King's voice was stern and commanding as he rebuked the impetuous bodyguards. "Allow the children to come to me. Don't forbid them, for my kingdom is made up largely of such as these."

Stunned by King Emmanuel's words, the two guards lowered the trembling boy to the ground and released him. "Come, Timothy," King Emmanuel said kindly, beckoning with gentle hands to the boy. "I would like to talk with you."

Timothy glanced up at the burly guards towering over him and then hurried to King Emmanuel's side. The King raised his voice. "Let all the children come to me!" he cried. "They are the important ones in my kingdom!"

With cries of joy, scores of children pulled free from their parents and ran to their King, who met them with outstretched arms. King Emmanuel knelt and began to hug the children around him, laughing and talking with them, touching them, stroking their hair. Timothy reached out and touched the King's beard, and the King laughed in delight. The children were thrilled at the attention showered upon them by the great monarch while their parents looked on in astonishment. Many of the dignitaries in the royal procession seemed annoyed at the interruption. A tall, dignified aid hurried to confer with the King. "But, sire," he said, "the heads of state are waiting!"

"Let them wait," King Emmanuel replied. "I'm talking with the children!"

Prince Josiah turned to the man beside him. "That's my King," he said proudly. "He always has time for the poor and needy!" He laughed. "Isn't that something? He makes the heads of state wait while he talks to the children of peasants!"

The man totally ignored Josiah, acting as if he had not heard a single word that Josiah had spoken. The young prince stared at the man, wondering why he was being so rude, and then he remembered that he was a visitor from another realm in time who could be neither seen nor heard. He sighed as he closed his book and found himself standing once again on the highly polished floor of the Library of Learning.

Josiah stepped to a second picture, opened his book to a particular page, and then stepped into the picture. At once he was standing in the center of an enormous great hall. Noticing groups of people clustered at one end of the vast room, he hurried in that direction. An enormous throne of gold stood upon a raised dais of ivory; upon the throne was the majestic personage of King Emmanuel. Josiah realized that His Majesty was holding court.

As Josiah watched, two guards dragged a prisoner before the King and dropped him to the floor less than five paces from the throne. The man's threadbare tunic told Josiah that the man was a peasant. A look of utter despair haunted the man's thin face, and Josiah felt a stab of sympathy.

"This man is accused of poaching, Your Majesty," Justice, the court recorder, reported in a stern voice that indicated the seriousness of the charge. Justice was a hard-faced man who looked as if he enjoyed bringing charges of wrongdoing against the populace. "He was caught red-handed, my Lord, with the carcass of a deer that he had slain upon the grounds of the castle. The arrow in the deer matched the others in this wretch's quiver, my Lord, so that there was no room for doubt as to the man's guilt."

He paused and consulted a document. "The penalty for poaching, Your Majesty, is death."

At these words the prisoner's head dropped and his shoulders sagged in despair. The recorder's pronouncement of the penalty seemed to take the very life out of the poor peasant.

"How do you plead?" King Emmanuel asked sternly.

"I am guilty, Your Majesty," the poacher replied in a thin, weak voice that trembled with emotion. "It is true—I did shoot the deer."

"Why did you shoot the deer," the King inquired, "knowing

that it belonged to me, and that the penalty for such theft was death?"

"I do not wish to excuse my actions, Your Majesty, but I shot the deer to feed my family. I cannot find work, sire, and my family has been without food for three days." Tears welled up in the man's eyes as he held up his hands to the King in a beseeching gesture. "I beg for pardon, Your Majesty, not for myself, but that you would be merciful to my family." Overcome with grief, the peasant fell on his face before the throne. "I am guilty as charged, my Lord, but I ask your forgiveness."

A deathly hush descended over the great hall. All eyes were upon King Emmanuel. The King sat silent for a long moment. "Release the prisoner," he ordered the guards. "The charges against him are dismissed."

The peasant let out his breath in a long, trembling sigh of relief coupled with a look of utter astonishment.

"But, sire, the penalty for this man's offense is death!" Justice protested. "He is a poacher! He has trespassed upon castle property and stolen from the royal herd. There is no question as to the man's guilt."

"The man has repented and asked forgiveness," King Emmanuel responded. "I have forgiven him, which is one thing that I always delight in doing."

He turned to an attendant standing nearby. "Never let it be said that a man in my kingdom would have to stoop to poaching to feed his family. Take provisions from the royal storehouse and then follow this man home. Once a week I want you to check with this family and determine that their needs are being met."

The pardoned poacher raised himself from the floor with a mixture of awe and gratitude written across his tear-stained face. "Your Majesty, I do not deserve this kindness! I thank you from the bottom of my heart."

The King smiled. "Go in peace, my son, for you are forgiven. But the next time a need arises within your family, tell me of your need."

Josiah found himself rubbing tears from his own eyes as he closed his book. His heart was full of love for his King.

Moments later the young prince entered a third picture to find that he was standing within a small, sparsely furnished room. A long table laden with the remains of a simple meal dominated the dimly lit chamber; resting around the table were nearly a dozen rugged-looking individuals. A servant was down upon his knees, washing the feet of one of the men.

Josiah watched as the humble servant removed the man's sandals, lifted one of his feet, and placed it in a basin of water on the floor. Using his bare hands, the servant scrubbed the dirt and grime from the other's foot. *What a disgusting task,* Josiah thought, *cleaning the feet of another person. I wouldn't trade places with that servant for anything.*

At that moment, the kneeling man turned his face in Josiah's direction. The young prince was shocked to recognize the face of King Emmanuel. His heart ached as he quietly closed the book.

Prince Josiah spent the next several days exploring in the Library of Learning. He visited volumes in all parts of the library, in both the New Wing and the Old, but his favorite volumes were the four in the New Wing that told of the life of King Emmanuel in Terrestria, and it was there that he spent most of his time. As he grew in the knowledge of his King, his love for the wise and loving monarch grew as well. His heart was full as he learned more and more of the greatness of his King.

"Have you visited the last volume in the New Wing?"

Student asked him one morning as he was heading to the Library of Learning for yet another day of study and discovery. "It's one of the most interesting of all, for it tells of the future of all Terrestria."

Josiah shook his head. "That's just about the only volume I haven't visited in the New Wing," he replied. "My favorites are the four volumes that tell of King Emmanuel's life, and that is where I have been spending most of my time. It's amazing what I have learned! I have seen my King as a servant, as a great teacher, and above all, as one who loves and forgives all who come to him. I even witnessed his death for me, though I could hardly bear to watch."

"The last volume reveals King Emmanuel in a way that no other volume does," Student told him. "Visit it today—I think you will be glad that you did."

Moments later Josiah paused before the last huge picture in the library. This volume somehow looked different from all the others. He couldn't place his finger on anything specific, but there was something about this one volume that set it apart from the other ones he had visited. He felt a deep sense of awe, almost a sense of foreboding, as he opened his book to the very last few pages. Taking a deep breath, he stepped into the picture.

The young prince found himself standing in the middle of a vast open space. At first he thought that he was in the outdoors—the place in which he stood was that immense—but as he looked about he slowly realized that he was inside a building that was so vast that he could see neither walls nor ceiling. Before him stood the largest gathering of people that he had ever seen in his life. There were millions of them—young and old, rich and poor, male and female, representatives from every color and race and region within Terrestria.

As Josiah studied the faces of those around him, he realized that the people were all waiting apprehensively for some great event to take place. Many, in fact, were weeping, and some wore a look of sheer terror upon their faces. Josiah wondered what was about to happen.

A great light emanated from a point far off in the distance, so the young prince made his way toward it. He had no trouble walking through the vast throng since he could pass right through the bodies of the people around him. No one seemed to notice or care as Josiah slipped through him or her. After a lengthy walk, he came within sight of a huge, powerful white throne that radiated the most intense white light that one could imagine. The beams of light from the great throne were so powerful that Josiah could not look at it for more than two or three seconds at a time.

Seated on the throne was a stern judge. He wore a robe of the purest white, which also radiated with the same pure light as the throne. Shielding his eyes with both hands, Josiah studied the face of the judge upon the great white throne. There was something strangely familiar about the man, but Josiah gave up trying to figure out what it was.

A powerful being dressed in shimmering white stood beside the throne. In his hands he held a huge scroll; beside him was a stand on which rested an enormous book. At a gesture from the judge, the attendant unrolled his scroll and called out a name. His voice echoed like thunder in the vast chamber.

As her name was called, a sobbing woman stepped forward and fell on her face before the throne. "Have mercy upon me, my Lord," she begged. "Have mercy!"

The judge turned to the tall figure with the scroll. "Is her name in the Book of the Redeemed?"

The attendant consulted the huge book, turning the pages

carefully and scanning the entries. Within seconds he had perused the entire book. "Her name does not appear, my Lord." The words were uttered with a tone of regret.

"I will do better, my Lord!" the woman sobbed. "Give me another chance!"

"You have lived a wicked life, and now is the day of your judgment. There is no second chance. You stand condemned."

The woman screamed. "Have mercy, my Lord, I beg you!"

"I am not your Lord, for you have never claimed me as such," the judge replied sternly, "and it is now too late for mercy. You have rejected my offers of mercy on countless occasions, and now the sentence of death is upon you."

The judge turned to the attendant with the scroll. "Send her to the Furnace of Eternal Fire." The woman let out a wail of terror and despair. Two attendants stepped forward and led her away.

Unrolling his scroll again, the attendant called out another name. A man stepped forward. He tried to stand tall, proud, and defiant, but at a single glance from the judge he fell trembling to the floor. When his name was not found recorded in the Book of the Redeemed, he, too, was led away weeping.

The judgment continued, with one person after another being called to stand before the unrelenting judge. Josiah watched the proceedings with a sense of dread. The judge's word was final; if a person's name did not appear in the huge record book, that person was sentenced to the eternal furnace, and there was no appeal. Watching the faces of the condemned, Josiah felt a terrific sense of remorse and sympathy for them, but at the same time he realized that the judge was being perfectly just. Suddenly he let out a little gasp as he recognized the man upon the powerful white throne. The judge was none other than King Emmanuel!

Someone touched Josiah's elbow, and he turned to see Student standing beside him. "It's a sobering scene, is it not, my prince?" the host said quietly. "This is an aspect of King Emmanuel's character that many fail to recognize: by his very nature, our King demands perfect justice." He sighed. "King Emmanuel is loving and gracious and forgiving, and sometimes because of his kindness people fail to see that he is also perfectly just. If they reject his mercy and pardon when he offers it, they must one day stand before him and be judged."

Josiah nodded, too overwhelmed to speak.

Student took him by the arm. "We have seen enough. Come, let us go." Josiah closed his book, and the vast courtroom vanished. Once again, Josiah and his friendly host were standing in the Library of Learning. Having witnessed the doom of countless fellow human beings, Josiah felt an overwhelming sense of sadness and loss.

"The time has come for you to leave the Castle of Knowledge," Student told Josiah as they walked across the vast New Wing of the library. "You have learned much about King Emmanuel, and now it is time for you to travel to the next castle."

"But sire, I want to stay here a while longer," Josiah pleaded. "I still have so much to learn! I have enjoyed my visits in the library, and it has been such a delight to learn about my King! Can I not stay a while longer, perhaps just a few days?"

"The purpose of the Castle of Knowledge is not to provide you with a complete knowledge of your King," Student answered, "for that could not be accomplished within a lifetime! Our purpose here is to create within you a hunger for knowledge of your King, to teach you the importance of wisdom and study. I think we have accomplished that goal, and now it is time for you to continue your quest."

"But my soul is hungry for knowledge of my King," Josiah protested. "I want to stay here. I want to learn more. Please allow me to stay! I want to visit the volumes that I have not yet fully explored."

"You can still do that after you leave the castle," Student told him quietly.

Josiah was puzzled. "How, sire?"

"You have the book. Open it each day and read it, and it will carry you in spirit to the same lands that you have been visiting these past few days. You have a lifetime ahead of you in which to learn more of your King."

He paused at the veil separating the two wings of the library and his eyes sparkled behind the thick lenses of his spectacles. "The next castle you will visit is the Castle of Temperance."

"What is temperance, sire?" Josiah asked.

"Temperance is control of self," the steward replied, "a very necessary character quality for a child of King Emmanuel. A man who cannot control self is like a city that is broken down, and without walls. We have prepared a horse for you to ride on this part of the journey, but I warn you—this will not be an easy journey. This part of your quest will try you as you have not been tried, and I pray that you will pass this test."

The morning sun reflected from the steward's hand with a brilliant flash of dazzling blue light, and Josiah saw that he was holding a magnificent sapphire. Kneeling before the young prince, Student touched the blazing jewel to Josiah's Shield of Faith, less than an inch from the emerald Josiah had received at the Castle of Virtue. The sapphire glowed brightly for a moment. When the castle steward released it, the gem was imbedded in the shield.

Student stood and placed a hand on the shoulder of the young prince. "Farewell, Prince Josiah. We have been honored by your visit to the Castle of Knowledge. May we wish you safety and success in your quest for the Castle of Temperance, in order that you may honor the name of our King."

Chapter Eleven

Prince Josiah turned in the saddle and looked back at the Castle of Knowledge nestled in the beautiful valley below. The castle was so tiny—how could it possibly have housed the vast Library of Learning? He shook his head in bewilderment. The tiny castle with its infinite library now held special memories for him. The countless hours of exploration within the volumes had greatly increased his knowledge of King Emmanuel and deepened his love for the great monarch.

Turning to the narrow trail that meandered into the forest, he urged his horse to a gentle canter. "This horse is named 'Hugo', my lord," the stablehand had told him as he saddled the tall roan stallion for Josiah. The boy had a speech impediment, and Josiah had struggled to understand him. "He is a bad horse, hard to control."

Josiah had laughed at the lad's attempts to warn him. "I've ridden hard-headed horses before," he had told the boy, confident in his own riding abilities. "I won't let him give me any trouble." He chuckled at the memory. Hugo had given him just a moment's argument when he first climbed into the saddle, tossing his head and bucking once or twice until Josiah had slapped him on the side of the neck with the reins. But after just one application of the reins, the roan had settled down immediately. "I guess you know who's in charge here, don't you, Hugo?" he said aloud.

Josiah rode along at any easy canter. The morning was cool but the sun was warm in the places where it shone through the trees to strike the earth in bright splashes of golden sunlight. From time to time the young prince caught a glimpse of the gentle dove as it flitted overhead above the trees. All went well until Josiah came to a fork in the trail. He reined Hugo to a stop and consulted his book to learn that he needed to take the trail to the right.

"Hurry along, Hugo," Josiah said, lifting the reins and guiding the horse to the right. But Hugo had ideas of his own. Tossing his head, he turned and took the trail to the left. He broke into a trot.

"Whoa, Hugo! Whoa!" Josiah shouted, pulling on the reins in an attempt to turn the horse around. "This is the wrong trail!" But the horse lowered his head and surged ahead, breaking into a run as if to show that he would not be controlled and would make his own decisions.

"Whoa!" Josiah stood in the stirrups and jerked back on the reins. The horse responded by turning from the trail and running at full speed through the forest. Josiah dropped back in the saddle and held on tight, ducking when overhanging branches threatened to unseat him. He pulled at the reins. "Whoa, Hugo! Whoa!"

The stubborn horse snorted, shook his head fiercely, and plunged ahead. Faster and faster he ran, darting around trees and leaping over fallen logs. The forest was darker here, and a small branch struck Josiah in the face before he even saw it. He lay forward against Hugo's neck to avoid being struck again as the runaway horse darted at full speed around one tree after another.

Moments later the forest floor swept up a hillside and Josiah's mount slowed as he climbed the steep slope. Josiah leaned back in the saddle to make it more difficult for the horse. Hugo turned and bit his leg.

Furious now, the young prince slashed at the stubborn horse with the end of the reins. Hugo bucked hard, nearly unseating him, and then wheeled around and plunged back down the slope. Josiah held on. When Hugo reached the bottom of the slope he came to an abrupt stop and stood trembling in every limb.

"You fool horse!" Josiah shouted, completely enraged by the horse's antics. "Now I don't even know where the trail is!"

"Let the horse have his head, my lord," a quiet voice suggested, and Josiah glanced over to see a tall stranger lounging in the shade of a willow.

"What do you mean, sire?" Josiah was trembling with rage.

"The horse knows the way—slack up on the reins and let him go the way that he wants. He'll get you where you want to go."

"Who are you, sire?"

"My name is Indulgence, and I know a thing or two about horses. The way you're going at it now, you'll be fighting that horse all day and never get anywhere. Let go of the reins and let him choose the path. He knows where to go."

"Are you sure, sire?"

The man laughed. "Do as you wish, my lord, but from where I stand I'd say that you'd be better off to quit trying to control that poor horse and let him have his head." He gave Josiah a strange look. "How did you get hitched up with such an ornery mount anyhow?"

"I chose him," Josiah said regretfully. "The stablehand was going to give me a mount named Meekness, but this one looked as if he had a bit more spirit, so I chose him."

Indulgence smiled and stepped away from the tree. "I'd say that you are in for a rough time," he said casually, strolling away through the trees as if to leave Josiah alone with his problem. "But you would do best to let the horse have his head! Let the reins go slack and just allow the horse to choose his own way. He knows these woods." Within a moment the man had disappeared among the trees.

Josiah sat still in the saddle for a moment or two as he pondered what to do with the troublesome horse. Hugo seemed determined to have his own way, and the young prince felt helpless to control him. Perhaps the stranger's advice was correct—if he simply allowed the ornery steed to choose his own way, maybe he would make his way to the Castle of Temperance on his own.

After another moment or two of thinking it over, Josiah sighed and dropped the reins on the back of the horse's neck. "Go on, Hugo," he said reluctantly, "choose your own path."

Hugo responded by trotting eagerly back in the direction from which he had come. Josiah was elated. It was working! In just a short while the horse and his young rider were back at the Path of Righteousness.

But to Josiah's dismay, Hugo turned and started down the trail in the wrong direction. Josiah reached for the reins, thought better of it, and simply sat back and waited. Hugo broke into a gallop. After traveling down the trail in the wrong direction for less than a furlong, the horse slowed when he came to a small farm. A crude wooden fence at the side of the trail surrounded a small, freshly plowed field. Tiny green shoots were just beginning to poke their eager heads through the soil. Hugo extended his neck over the fence and began to eat the tender young plants.

Josiah was frustrated. He shook the reins. "Hugo," he scolded, "this is not what you are supposed to do. You are supposed to take me to the Castle of Temperance. Get moving!"

Hugo just snorted, shook his head belligerently, and continued to graze.

Josiah waited impatiently, uncertain as to what to do. Indulgence seemed like a knowledgeable man; he had advised letting the horse choose his own way, and yet that plan didn't seem to be working. He sighed. Perhaps if he simply let the obstinate horse feed for a few moments unhindered, he would soon feel like traveling in the right direction.

Several hours later, Hugo was still grazing. He had eaten every plant in the field within reach of the path, and now he was consuming the wild grass that grew along the other side of the trail. Realizing that he had made a huge mistake in allowing the ornery horse to choose his own path, Prince Josiah finally pulled back firmly on the reins, raised his heels, and kicked Hugo in the flanks. The troublesome horse snorted and shook his head angrily, turned and looked at Josiah, and then went back to grazing.

"This has gone far enough, Hugo," the young prince declared firmly. He tugged the reins fiercely to one side, turning the horse's head back to the trail. "You are not taking me to the Castle of Temperance as you are supposed to; you are simply choosing what you want to do, and I've had enough of this nonsense. Right now, I'm taking charge, and you are going to obey me! We're going to the Castle of Temperance! Now get moving!" Raising both feet, Josiah brought his heels down against Hugo's flanks with all his might.

In the next instant Josiah found himself sailing over the fence to land face first in the plowed soil of the field. Hugo had bucked him off!

Unhurt by the fall but angered by the horse's actions, Josiah leaped to his feet. "You blackguard!" he raged at the horse. "I'll teach you a thing or two!" But he turned around just in time to see Hugo gallop away through the trees. The horse had left him stranded.

Josiah was furious. "You worthless, good for nothing animal!" he raged, kicking at the fence with all his might. His booted foot struck the fence post, doing no damage to the post, but sending a spasm of pain through his foot and making him angrier still. Roaring in pain, he drew back his fist and punched the fence, hurting his hand. Clutching his injured hand and hopping about on one foot, Josiah howled in pain.

When the pain in his hand and foot had subsided somewhat, the angry young prince climbed over the fence and stood in the middle of the trail. *There's no sense in chasing that churlish horse,* he decided. *He won't take me where I need to go, anyway. I might as well start walking again!* Seething with anger, Josiah turned and started down the trail.

The young prince let out a long sigh of frustration. He picked up a long stick in the trail and swung it angrily at tree branches as he walked along. "I thought I would get to enjoy this part of the journey," he said aloud, although no one was around to listen to him. He swatted angrily at a small bush beside the trail, scattering tiny red berries left and right. "I was going to get to ride in comfort, instead of having to walk. And what happens?" He took another angry swing at a milkweed plant. "I get some dunderhead horse that doesn't even know enough to follow directions, and he throws me. Here I am walking, instead of riding. And all because I chose the wrong horse!"

He walked in angry silence for several moments. With each step he took, he stabbed furiously at the ground with the stick. High overhead, clouds crept in front of the sun. Shadows fell across the forest, but Josiah failed to notice.

"Why did I even come on this quest anyway?" he muttered. "All I do is walk and walk. Here I am, Prince Josiah, walking like a common servant. I suppose it will take all day to walk to the Castle of Temperance."

He spotted a bird's nest in a thorn bush beside the trail and gave it a whack with the stick. "If King Emmanuel really cared about me, he would have provided me a fine horse to ride, not some old nag like Hugo." He sighed, suddenly feeling misused and unwanted. "The King rides in a golden carriage, and I walk."

Josiah kicked at a rock in the trail, stubbing his toe and wincing in pain. "It's Student's fault," he pouted. "He should have seen to it that I had a fine horse to ride, instead of a stubborn steed like that miserable Hugo. But does he care? He just lets me choose a horse by myself, knowing full well that I didn't know anything about that stable of horses. Why didn't he help me?"

The young prince looked around with a growing sense of dismay. The forest was dark and gloomy here; the trees were gnarled and twisted, stunted specimens that sagged and drooped over the narrow trail like crippled old men. Blotches of dark moss hung from their shriveled limbs like tattered clothing. The air was dank and chill, and reeked of decay; the trail was wet and slippery. Without realizing it, Josiah had left the trail to the Castle of Temperance and wandered into the Forest of Self-Pity, perhaps one of the most treacherous regions in all of Terrestria. After a number of joy-filled days at the Castle of Knowledge experiencing blessing and growth as he learned of his King, in an hour's time he had become a grumbling, defeated young man who was consumed with ingratitude and self-pity.

Josiah's melancholy mood continued to worsen as he walked

along through the gloom of the dark forest. "No one cares about me," he muttered. "Student didn't care! Why didn't he give me a better horse? Why did he allow me to select a horse that was going to give me trouble? Why didn't Sir Faithful warn me about things like this? Why did King Emmanuel send me on such a treacherous journey, anyway? Why couldn't I have stayed at the Castle of Faith? I was happy there! Why do I have to tramp from castle to castle like a homeless troubadour? Why couldn't I have stayed a while longer at the Castle of Knowledge? I had such a splendid time there."

The forest grew darker.

Realizing that he had not seen the dove for some time, Josiah glanced around, but the snowy white form of his celestial guide was nowhere to be seen. The wind howled mournfully through the twisted trees, moaning one moment and screeching the next as if it resented the presence of the young prince. Josiah shivered and drew his cloak more tightly about him. Fear grew within him. For just a moment he considered retracing his steps to the Castle of Knowledge to seek help, but he quickly put the thought behind him and pushed resolutely onward. He would make it on his own. Was it his fault that the dove had chosen to desert him?

The trail became narrower. Brambles and briars clutched at his clothing as he passed. The trees seemed to reach for him, snatching at his arms and face with withered, gnarled branches as if they were determined to hold him back. He gasped for breath as he stumbled along in the darkness and gloom. Discouraged and angry, he failed to realize the danger of his situation.

Soon the trees of the forest gave way to stunted shrubs, twisted thorn bushes and creeping vines. Clumps of sharp-bladed sawgrass and thorny briars appeared along the trail.

The ground was soggy and spongy, oozing brackish water with Josiah's every step. The air had become bitter and foul, stinging his eyes and searing his throat. Josiah struggled to breathe, rubbing his burning eyes as he stumbled along. Poisonous vapors swirled across the trail, making him dizzy and nauseous, disoriented and confused.

Hearing a raucous screech, he looked up just in time to see a dark, squawking bird of prey diving at his head. He swung the stick with all his might, striking the attacking fowl and driving it away. He walked faster.

Steaming mud pots on both sides of the trail bubbled and hissed, releasing little clouds of noxious vapors into the air. Josiah's eyes burned so fiercely that he could barely keep them open. He struggled to breathe. The trail became even narrower, and soon was nothing more than a series of steppingstones crossing a swampy morass that bubbled and simmered like a witch's brew.

Josiah's careless steps had taken him into the Swamp of Bitterness, a place so deadly that it had claimed the life and health of countless pilgrims before him. He struggled to jump from steppingstone to steppingstone, unaware of the danger he was in, never realizing that the safest course of action would have been to retrace his steps to firmer ground. Had he been more alert, he would have noticed the countless white skeletons that protruded from the muck and mire, silent witnesses to the treachery of the swamp in which he found himself. As he passed a thorn bush beside the trail, a venomous snake with white death markings on its head dropped into the murky water and slithered away unnoticed.

Angry squawks drew his attention to the sky as a pair of dark vultures swooped down upon him. With wings spread wide and talons extended, the foul birds darted back and forth repeatedly, slashing at his face and neck with their beaks and claws in an attempt to knock him from the trail. Raising his hands to protect his head, the young prince stumbled forward.

One of the vultures raked the side of his face with a sharp claw. Josiah stumbled, lost his balance, and fell forward, missing his footing on the next steppingstone. With a cry of dismay, he tumbled from the path to land in the bubbling, hissing mire of the Swamp of Bitterness.

Chapter Twelve

Prince Josiah lay in the sulfurous mud of the Swamp of Bitterness, stunned by his fall from the Path of Righteousness. The weight of his own bitterness pulled him down as the brackish water and putrid slime of the swamp began to close over him. He struggled frantically, thrashing about and reaching desperately for a handhold on solid ground. But his grasping fingers simply came up with handfuls of the disgusting muck and slime of the swamp. Within seconds he was submerged to the waist and sinking deeper every moment.

The Swamp of Bitterness pulled at his limbs and clothing with a vicious suction, drawing him deeper into the mire inch by inch. It was as if the swamp were a living thing determined to pull him under and snuff out his life. Summoning all of his strength, Josiah lunged against the unrelenting suction and reached as far as he could. His frantic fingers closed around a clump of grass at the edge of the trail, and he grasped the vegetation desperately, knowing that if he lost his grip the swamp would take him under. "Help!" he cried aloud. "Somebody, please help me!"

The vile mud crept higher and higher. He was now submerged nearly to his armpits.

The young prince could feel the strength ebbing from his weary hands and arms, and he knew that it was simply a matter of time before he lost his grip on the clump of grass and the unrelenting Swamp of Bitterness pulled him under. He raised his head and gasped for breath. "Help me!" Hearing the flutter of wings, he looked up hopefully. His heart sank when he saw the dark form of a hideous vulture. The loathsome fowl dropped into the twisted skeleton of a dead tree and settled down to watch him. Josiah shuddered. His head sank in despair, drooping lower and lower until his face was almost in the vile slime. The muck and mire had now closed over his shoulders; only his arms and head were visible above the surface of the swamp. Within moments the Swamp of Bitterness would consume another victim.

"Lad, are you alive?" The voice was like a bolt of lightning in its abruptness, and Josiah looked up. Standing above him on the steppingstones was the figure of a nobleman dressed in a splendid doublet of royal blue with a cloak of scarlet. His eyes were filled with concern.

"Can you help me, sire?" Josiah gasped weakly. "The swamp is about to pull me under!"

"I am Lord Thankful, Earl of Gratitude," the man replied. "I heard your cries for assistance and came to see if I may be of help."

"Pull me out, please, Lord Thankful," Josiah begged. "I cannot hold on much longer!"

"I cannot pull you out," the nobleman told him, "for no man can pull another out of the Swamp of Bitterness. But I can tell you how to get out."

"Tell me quickly," Josiah begged. "I am about to be pulled under!"

"Praise," Lord Thankful said simply. "Praise will get you out."

"Praise, sire?" Josiah repeated.

"Aye, my young friend, praise. Lift your voice in praise to King Emmanuel, and the Swamp of Bitterness will lose its power over you. But make haste, for I can see that you have precious little time left."

The murky water and foul slime had now reached to Josiah's chin. With an unearthly slurping noise, the swamp was taking him down faster and faster. Josiah was terrified. Straining upward against the unrelenting suction, he gasped for breath. "Help me, Lord Thankful!" he pleaded. Releasing his feeble hold on the clump of grass, he lifted his right hand toward the nobleman. "Help me, sire!"

"Praise, lad, praise!" Lord Thankful shouted. "Praise the mighty name of your King, and the Swamp of Bitterness will lose its power over you! Praise the name of King Emmanuel!"

The filthy water of the swamp had now closed over Josiah's mouth. In desperation, he threw back his head and lifted his chin, gulping a deep lungful of precious air. His mind raced. Praise? How could he praise his King? In his moment of hopelessness, the words of a familiar song flooded his soul and then burst from his lips.

"I sing the greatness of my King, my Lord Emmanuel," he sang, in a voice that trembled with fear and desperation. "His power is great and far exceeds what mortal tongue or pen can tell." Gasping for breath, he finished the stanza: "My heart is full; I sing for him, and trust that I may serve him well."

He stopped and looked about him. The Swamp of Bitterness still held him fast, but he had stopped sinking.

"Sing, lad, sing!" Lord Thankful called urgently. "Praise the name of your King!"

"I sing the love of my great King, my Lord Emanuel," Josiah sang. "His lovingkindness ransomed me, but why he did, I cannot tell." The mire was actually receding now, falling slowly from his shoulders as if he were rising from the swamp.

"Sing, lad, sing!"

"His love led him to die for me. I trust that I may serve him well." There was no doubt about it; the mire of the foul swamp was definitely receding.

"Sing it again, lad, sing it again!" Lord Thankful urged. "Keep praising your King until the swamp loses its power over you!"

Josiah sang. The bitterness and ingratitude flowed from his soul like water pouring from a bucket. The dreadful feelings were replaced by a warm, grateful peace. Once again, his heart was filled with love for his King. He looked about in astonishment. The foul swamp with its noxious, bitter vapors was gone; he found himself standing on firm ground, surrounded by luscious green grass, colorful flowers and blossoming trees. "What happened to the swamp?" he asked Lord Thankful.

"The Swamp of Bitterness is a treacherous, dangerous place, my prince, but it has no power over a child of the King who has a heart full of praise. Gratitude and praise will vanquish bitterness every time."

"Sire, you came just in time," Josiah said gratefully. "I was about to perish in that foul place!"

"How did you come to fall into the swamp?" the nobleman asked. "That was no place for a child of the King."

"I am Prince Josiah, of the Castle of Faith," the young prince replied, "and I am on my way to the Castle of Temperance. I was riding a horse named 'Hugo' that I chose from the stable at the Castle of Knowledge, and he threw me! I started walking and somehow wandered into that dreadful swamp."

"Hugo?" The look on Lord Thankful's face was one of bewilderment. "Where did you find a horse named 'Hugo'?"

"He was in the stable at the Castle of Knowledge. The

stablehand wanted to give me a mount named 'Meekness', but I made a horrible mistake and chose Hugo."

Lord Thankful began to laugh. "Ego! Your horse's name was 'Ego'!"

"Ego?" Josiah echoed. "But the stablehand told me the horse's name was 'Hugo'."

The nobleman laughed again. "The stablehand does not speak clearly. The horse's name was 'Ego'. It's an ancient word that means 'self'. One of the hardest lessons for a child of the King to learn—and one of the most important—is control of self."

Josiah dropped to a seat on a nearby rock. He was still breathing hard from his ordeal in the Swamp of Bitterness. "Control of self. Student told me that's what temperance is—control of self. You must know that I'm on my way to the Castle of Temperance."

Lord Thankful nodded.

At that moment the dove fluttered down to alight in the branches of a nearby tree. Josiah glanced at his feathered guide and then looked back to Lord Thankful. "Why did he desert me in my time of greatest need?" he asked.

"Oh, he would never desert you," the nobleman assured him. "He is with you always. But in your anger, ingratitude, and bitterness, you were simply unaware of his presence. He would have helped you, had you listened for his voice. In fact, he could have given you complete control over Ego."

Prince Josiah hung his head.

"Come, my prince, let us make our way to the Castle of Temperance. I am the castle steward, and I have been awaiting your arrival. The castle is not far."

The Castle of Temperance was a concentric castle situated on the banks of Distinction River, the watercourse that divided the Plains of Integrity, a rich, well-watered region, from the Morass of Gratification, a place filled with sulfur pits and treacherous bogs. Prince Josiah spent several days at the castle. Lord Thankful was a gracious host and made him feel welcome. Josiah was grateful for the many kindnesses showed to him, not the least of which was the fact that the nobleman never again mentioned the fact that Josiah had failed to control Ego and had ended up in the Swamp of Bitterness. The young prince spent countless hours reading and studying his book and was delighted to discover that his knowledge of King Emmanuel increased just as rapidly as it had during his time at the Castle of Knowledge.

Lord Thankful stressed the importance of daily praise and thanksgiving in order to maintain a heart of gratitude and avoid the perils of allowing bitterness to creep into one's heart and soul. Having experienced the Swamp of Bitterness for himself, Josiah had no desire to return. He began each day in the castle with a time set aside to read his book and to reflect on King Emmanuel's goodness to him. Throughout the day he found himself singing the King's praises again and again. From time to time he sent petitions to Emmanuel just to express his gratitude for his deliverance from the tyranny of Argamor and from the chains of iniquity.

"The next stop in your journey is the Castle of Patience," the castle steward told him after breakfast one morning. "Today you shall resume your quest and make your way toward that castle."

Josiah nodded in agreement. "I am ready, sire."

Lord Thankful led the young prince to the main gate of the castle. "Patience is determination," he told Josiah, "the ability to keep going when difficulties or obstacles arise. It's also referred to as 'persistence' or 'steadfastness', and this next part of the journey will test you in regard to that aspect of your character. The Mountains of Difficulty lay across your route, and the crossing will not be an easy one. Allow your book and the dove to guide you and you will do fine. Trust in Emmanuel's love for you, and petition him if you find yourself in dire circumstances."

An attendant appeared just then with a pack of provisions for Josiah. "Food for your journey," Lord Thankful told Josiah.

Josiah took the pack and slipped his arms into the straps, amazed at the weight of the pack. "How much food is in this?" he asked. A troubling thought suddenly occurred to him, and he turned to the steward. "Will I not reach the Castle of Patience by nightfall? Judging by the weight of this pack, I would venture to guess that there is food enough here for several days."

Lord Thankful nodded. "This leg of the journey will be the longest yet," he agreed. "The trek across the Mountains of Difficulty will not be an easy one, nor will it be a brief one. But King Emmanuel has provided everything that you will need for the journey. The trail follows Distinction River northward for about twenty-five or thirty furlongs and then turns east toward the Mountains of Difficulty. Whatever you do, Prince Josiah, stay on the trail! There are no shortcuts through the mountains, so don't leave the Path of Righteousness for any reason whatsoever. To do so would be to invite disaster."

Reaching within his royal blue doublet, the steward took out a small drawstring bag. He opened it and dumped a large, beautiful ruby into the palm of his hand. Lifting the young prince's Shield of Faith with one hand, he stooped slightly and held the crimson red jewel to the shield in a line with the emerald and the sapphire. The ruby glowed for an instant with a brilliant red light as it became part of the shield.

Lord Thankful smiled. "Farewell, Prince Josiah. It has been a joy to have you with us in the Castle of Temperance these last few days."

Two hours later Josiah strolled over the top of a gentle ridge and stared in amazement. Before him stretched a series of rugged mountains. Tall, stark, and jagged, the Mountains of Difficulty loomed ahead like a series of formidable castles. The mountains were so high that in some places the peaks pierced the clouds.

Josiah paused in the middle of the trail and took a deep breath. Lord Thankful was right—the trek across the Mountains of Difficulty was not going to be an easy crossing. Setting his shoulders in determination, the young prince boldly strode forward.

"Wait, my lord!"

Prince Josiah turned. A youth just a year or two older than he was running up the trail toward him.

"Might I accompany you on your journey, my lord?" the youth asked as he caught up with Josiah. "The Mountains of Difficulty can be quite treacherous at times, my lord, and it is best not to traverse them alone." He bent over and leaned on his knees with both hands, breathing hard.

"I shall be glad for your company," Josiah replied. "As soon as you have had time to catch your breath, we shall resume our journey."

"I am called by the name of Woebegone," the youth said.

"And I am Prince Josiah, of the Castle of Faith," the young prince answered. "I am pleased to make your acquaintance."

"I am ready to travel," Woebegone said just a moment later. "Shall we be off?"

Josiah studied his new companion as he and Woebegone hiked along the trail. The young man was extremely thin, his tunic nearly threadbare and his sandals were so worn that they appeared that they would fall apart at any moment. He wore a sad, doleful expression; his dark eyes revealed a haunted, fearful spirit.

The sunshine was bright and the day was cheery, but Josiah couldn't help noticing that Woebegone kept eyeing the distant mountains with a timid, almost terrified look. The young prince began to wonder what lay ahead.

Chapter Thirteen

The rocky trail upon which Prince Josiah and Woebegone traveled angled sharply up into the mountains. Josiah paused and looked upward. High above them, the steep mountain trail wound its way along the very edge of a sheer precipice. A fall from the trail would certainly prove fatal. Spotting movement on the side of the mountain well above the tree line, Josiah pointed. "Look. Is that another traveler?"

"Indeed it is," Woebegone replied. "We'll reach that point where he is in a day or two."

"A day or two?" Josiah's heart sank at the words. If it took a full day to reach that point, the trip through the mountains might take a month or more. Josiah's enthusiasm sagged at the thought. "Well, let's keep traveling, shall we?"

Woebegone shrugged listlessly and started forward.

Josiah began to sing, but Woebegone cut him off. "Save your breath," he advised. "You'll need it for the climb."

Josiah laughed. "Why are you so glum?"

"You'd be glum, too, my lord," Woebegone answered, "if you only knew what lies ahead."

Josiah hesitated. "What do you mean?"

"Crossing the Mountains of Difficulty is no easy feat, my

lord. Many a traveler has perished in the mountains that lie before us."

"Why? What can happen?"

"There are wild animals that prey upon travelers. Countless people have been killed and eaten by lions or wolves or bears." He eyed Josiah's splendid clothing. "And it matters not whether one is a prince or a pauper, my lord; the wild animals will attack anyone."

"I feel no fear," Josiah replied, reaching within his doublet and drawing the book. "I have my sword." He swung the book, transforming it into the invincible sword.

Woebegone's eyes grew wide at the sight of the glittering blade, but he quickly recovered. "There are winds so fierce that they can pluck a man from the mountainside and hurl him to his death. The winds are swift, and strike without warning."

"Trust in your King, Prince Josiah," the dove said softly.

"I'm trusting in King Emmanuel," Josiah said resolutely. "The fierce winds do not alarm me."

"There are many rockslides and avalanches," Woebegone warned him. "As we climb you will see countless places where the entire trail has fallen away. The mountainside is treacherous, and can crumble away before you even know what's happening." He paused, eyeing Josiah carefully. "And it is rumored that the mountains are home to a fierce dragon— a huge, fire-breathing monster that preys on travelers."

The trail grew steeper and narrower. Josiah crept to the edge and cautiously looked down. Already the valley floor was more than two hundred feet below them. Woebegone stood behind him and nudged him forward slightly with his shoulder, startling Josiah and causing him to draw back from the edge of the precipice. "It would be easy to fall to one's death, my lord. You must be careful."

Together the two youths resumed their journey up the side of the mountain. "The crossing will take days and days, my lord," Woebegone continued. "The air is thin; the nights are cold and the days are hot. It will not be an easy journey, my lord. Perhaps you would want to turn back while you still have the opportunity."

Josiah laughed. "Don't you have any good news for me?"

"Well, there is one good thing," Woebegone said slowly.

"What's that?"

"Death in the mountains usually comes quickly, so at least one does not have to worry about a lingering death."

"Thank you," Josiah told him. "That was encouraging."

The young prince and his pessimistic companion climbed steadily. In less than an hour they found themselves above the tree line and Josiah realized that they had already passed the point at which he had seen the traveler above them, but he said nothing to Woebegone. The rugged trail continually grew steeper and more treacherous. Josiah hiked cautiously, fully realizing that a misstep could result in a fatal fall to the valley below.

The worst part of the journey was Woebegone's endless prattle—he went on and on about the dangers ahead and the possibilities of a sudden and unexpected death. He complained about the weather and the climbing conditions. He suggested that Josiah could not possibly have enough food in his pack for the entire trek across the mountains, and that death by starvation was a very real possibility. He continually told Josiah that as bad as things were now, he should keep in mind that the worst was still yet to come—the higher elevations were the most treacherous of all. Josiah soon grew weary of the constant barrage of negative information.

By midday they had reached the crest of the first mountain range. After a brief rest break to eat a meal from Josiah's pack, they started down the backside of the ridge. The sun was hotter now, but the incline was gentler and the trail was now downhill. Josiah found comfort in the fact that they were no longer hiking along the edge of a precipice.

The sun was setting when the two travelers came to a small log cabin nestled in a grove of tall pine trees. Crystal-clear water bubbled from a spring in the rocks beside the cabin and flowed down the mountainside along a rocky bed. "Behold," Josiah told Woebegone, "here's a place to spend the night!"

Woebegone shook his head. "We know not who owns the cabin," he said, with a woeful expression on his thin face. "We dare not stay here without permission."

Noticing a brass plate upon the door of the cabin, Josiah stepped closer. ***"WELCOME, WEARY TRAVELER,"*** the brass plate proclaimed in large letters. ***"THIS HAVEN OF REFUGE IS OPEN TO ANY AND ALL WHO DESIRE A PLACE OF REST. THIS SHELTER IS PROVIDED BY HIS MAJESTY, KING EMMANUEL."***

Josiah opened the door. "Come," he called to Woebegone. "The cabin has been provided for us by King Emmanuel." Stepping inside, the young prince surveyed the interior of the cabin. Four bunks prepared with sweet-smelling pine branches lined the walls; an axe and a box of kindling stood to one side of a clean, well-swept fireplace. The mantel above the fireplace held a lantern, a flint, and a small tinderbox.

"I see no provisions of victuals," Woebegone said, standing in the doorway and looking about the little cabin with an expression of disdain. "The King did not provide victuals for us. If he really cared for us he would have provided for our needs."

Josiah shook his head. "I brought food in my pack," he told his complaining companion. "King Emmanuel has already provided it."

"The cabin will be freezing tonight," Woebegone lamented. "The Mountains of Difficulty are bitterly cold at night."

"That's why King Emmanuel has provided a fireplace," Josiah pointed out. "I will take the axe and cut some firewood."

"There is no lock on the door," Woebegone complained. "Someone could enter the cabin while we are asleep and slay us in our beds."

"Would you rather sleep outside?" Josiah retorted, beginning to grow tired of his companion's constant whining. "The cabin is open to all, but it will keep the wild animals out." He picked up the axe and strode to the door. "I'm going to cut some firewood. Why don't you prepare the kindling so we can start a fire when I get back?"

Moments later Josiah found a dead tree on the mountainside above the cabin. In no time at all he had cut a good supply of firewood. He returned to the cabin with a huge armload of wood to find that Woebegone had done nothing to prepare a fire. Clenching his teeth to hold back the angry words that threatened to leap out, the young prince knelt and built a fire.

He picked up his pack, noticing as he did that the pack seemed much lighter than before. "What happened?" he asked. "Some of my food seems to be missing."

"Much of the food was starting to mold and decay," Woebegone told him, "so I threw it over the precipice below the cabin."

Josiah stared at him in disbelief.

"We must turn back tomorrow," the mournful youth insisted. "There is not enough food for the journey. There is no food to be found in the Mountains of Difficulty. We will perish with hunger!"

"Turn back if you so desire," Josiah told him. "I shall continue on without you. I'm on a quest for my King, and I will not turn back!"

Woebegone shrugged and said nothing.

The next few days were difficult ones indeed. The Path of Righteousness seemed to grow steeper and more treacherous every day as the youths followed it through the Mountains of Difficulty. In many respects, Woebegone's dire warnings had proved to be accurate—the journey was becoming more difficult. The trail was dangerous; the days were hot; and the nights were cold. On some days, the winds of adversity howled down from the mountain peaks from morning till night. Rockslides and avalanches were frequent, and on occasion, Josiah even spotted the skeletons of other travelers who had perished on the journey.

A constant burden during the trek through the Mountains of Difficulty was Woebegone's constant message of doom and gloom. It seemed that he could hardly open his mouth without predicting failure, or even worse, death. Josiah chose to ignore the words of woe. In spite of the fact that Woebegone had thrown much of the King's provisions of food into the ravine the first night, Josiah noticed that the pack never grew lighter after that first night. It was as if King Emmanuel was somehow supplying their needs by replenishing the food as they ate it. He had also noticed that each and every night, just as the sun was going down, he and Woebegone would come to one of the King's cabins of rest. The cabins had somehow been placed in the very places where they were needed most.

"Look at this," Woebegone said, pausing at a place where a rockslide had destroyed the trail. "This precipice is more than a thousand feet high! One misstep here, and we're dead men!"

"Cross it carefully," Josiah replied. "We'll be all right."

"Don't look down," Woebegone told him, stepping closer to the place of danger. "If you see how far it is to the bottom, you'll be paralyzed with fear!" Moving slowly and carefully, he began to inch his way across the breach in the trail. The young prince followed cautiously.

"Do you think that King Emmanuel knows that this trail is this treacherous?" Woebegone asked slyly.

"I'm sure he does," Josiah replied. He glanced downward at that moment and his heart constricted with fear. It *was* a long way to the bottom.

"Why do you think that your King would send you into such a place of danger?" Woebegone continued. "Surely it is not because he cares for you! Perhaps you are not as valuable to him as you had thought—perhaps he sees you as merely another of his many servants, and you are expendable to him."

"King Emmanuel cares for me!" Josiah retorted hotly. "I'm more to him than just a servant. He adopted me into the Royal Family. I'm his son and his heir."

Woebegone shrugged and turned toward Josiah, smiling for the first time since the two had been together. "Perhaps, my lord. But if that is true, why would the King send you into a place of such danger?"

Josiah couldn't answer. Woebegone's words troubled him. Would King Emmanuel actually have sent him on this quest, knowing that he would have to face the dangers of the Mountains of Difficulty, if he really cared for Josiah? *What if I perish in these mountains? Will King Emmanuel know about it? Will he even care?* Josiah tried to put such thoughts out of his head, but they kept returning again and again.

They encountered yet another difficulty on the sixth day. It was late in the afternoon, and Woebegone was leading the way through a steep mountain pass. As Josiah stepped around a large pile of jagged boulders that blocked the trail, he found the thin youth standing in the middle of the path, staring up the trail in dismay. "Now we really have trouble," Woebegone moaned. "Look! Snow!"

Patches of crusty snow lined both sides of the trail. "It's just a little bit," Josiah pointed out. "Look, the trail is still clear."

Woebegone gave him a look of disgust. "You don't understand, do you? The snow is no trouble here, but we still have to climb another two thousand feet before we make it over the pass. At that altitude the snow will be blocking the trail. We'll freeze to death before we make it over the mountain!"

Josiah shrugged. "The only thing to do is to keep hiking and trust in our King."

Woebegone started forward. "King Emmanuel should have provided us with warmer clothing if we are to travel in conditions such as this."

The afternoon grew colder as they struggled steadily upward. The air was thin, and Josiah panted with the exertion of climbing. Woebegone, for all his grumbling and complaining, seemed unaffected by the altitude or the cold and climbed without effort. Josiah struggled to keep up. Before long he noticed that he could actually see his own breath in the cold mountain air.

As they reached the higher elevations, they saw more and more snow. Parts of the trail were icy and completely covered with snow, and soon they were trudging through snow that was more than a foot deep. The Path of Righteousness was indistinct and hard to follow.

Why did King Emmanuel not provide us with warmer clothing? Josiah asked himself repeatedly. *Did he not know that we would face such climbing conditions? Did he not care? Is Woebegone right—does King Emmanuel view me as nothing more than a servant? Am I expendable?* Josiah felt disloyal even thinking such thoughts, but for some reason, found that he could no longer chase them from his mind.

Woebegone spoke up. "We're going to find ourselves facing a major problem tonight."

"What is that?" Josiah asked.

"We're far above the tree line. When we get to the cabin—ah, if there is a cabin—what are we going to do for firewood? We'll freeze to death!"

Josiah thought about the problem as he hiked along, forcing his way through snowdrifts that were waist deep. He watched the sun dropping quickly toward the peaks in the west and he knew that night was almost upon them. Surely there would be a cabin—there had been one at just the right location every night so far—but what *would* they do for firewood? He worried about it, and fear tugged at his heart.

There was less than fifteen minutes of daylight left when they finally came in sight of the cabin, a sturdy little structure less than two hundred paces below the summit of the mountain. Prince Josiah hiked faster and passed Woebegone on the trail. "There's not a tree within several miles of here," the dismal youth pointed out to the prince for the ninth or tenth time. "We'll freeze to death!"

Josiah was running now, leaping high with each step in his battle against the deep snow. He scrambled up the last few paces to the cabin and threw open the door. The interior of the cabin was dark, and it was hard to see. He took a timid step inside and blinked, waiting for his eyes to grow accustomed to the dim light. His heart leaped. Just as in the other cabins, a fireplace was waiting, with flint and tinder and kindling and all the necessary items for building a fire. But there was no axe. Instead, one entire wall was stacked from floor to ceiling with seasoned firewood!

"You were wrong!" Josiah told Woebegone, as the latter stepped into the cabin. "Look at all the firewood! King Emmanuel *did* provide for us!"

Three days later, Prince Josiah and Woebegone carefully descended the last rugged incline. The treacherous crossing was nearly over; the Mountains of Difficulty were behind them. At the base of the mountain was one last rugged canyon that they would have to cross; beyond that stretched a wide, flat plain. Josiah could see a castle far in the distance, and he knew without asking that it was the Castle of Patience. This part of the journey was nearly over.

"We'll cut across that ledge just below us," Woebegone told him, pointing to a sandstone promontory below the trail. The trail doubles back just below there, and we'll save ourselves a bit of walking."

"Lord Thankful cautioned me about leaving the trail," Josiah countered. "I think we should follow it all the way down."

Woebegone snorted. "We're past the treacherous part now," he argued. "The trail goes on another two or three furlongs and then doubles back on itself to a point just a few feet below. There's no sense in walking an extra four or five furlongs when there's no reason for it."

With these words he stepped from the trail and began to hike straight down the side of the mountain. Josiah hesitated for a moment, and then, with a shrug, followed Woebegone.

The side of the ridge was covered with outcroppings of loose rock that broke away easily when Josiah used them for handholds or footholds. Realizing that his situation was precarious, Josiah proceeded slowly and cautiously, testing each rocky spur before he trusted his weight to it. *Perhaps I should have simply followed the trail,* he told himself ruefully.

He stepped down on a fist-sized projection of rock and it broke away without warning. Josiah found himself sliding feet first down the steep slope. He rolled over on his belly and scrabbled desperately for a handhold to stop his fall, but his clutching fingers simply encountered more loose rock. He slid faster and faster. With a cry of fear he dropped over the edge of a precipice and found himself falling through empty space. Barely a second later, he struck the rocky floor of the canyon and his world went black.

Chapter Fourteen

The fog began to clear from Prince Josiah's mind. Slowly he became aware of his surroundings. He lifted his head and looked around—he discovered that he was lying on his back in the rugged canyon. Thirty feet above him, Woebegone peered at him from a rocky ledge.

The young prince slowly rolled to his feet and stood up. He stretched his limbs and took a quick inventory. Apparently, nothing was broken. He looked up at his companion. "I'm all right!" he called. "But how do I get out of this canyon?"

To his astonishment, Woebegone began to laugh hysterically. "You don't get out, my lord!" he cried, doubled over in fits of uncontrolled laughter. His voice echoed and re-echoed in the canyon. "This is the Valley of Discouragement, and there is no escape. You will never get out, my lord. Others before you have tried, but you will find their bleached bones down there with you!" He turned away.

"Wait!" Josiah cried. "Help me out!"

The thin youth turned back with a sneering laugh. "Help you out of the Valley of Discouragement?" he echoed. "Surely you jest, my lord. You are right where we want you."

Josiah was desperate. "Then send someone who can help

me!" he pleaded.

The only answer was the mocking laugh that echoed back and forth across the canyon. Woebegone darted up the trail and was gone.

Josiah looked around with a growing sense of dismay. An unusual twilight seemed to hang over the Valley of Discouragement like a translucent shroud; the mountainside above the valley was brightly lit and he could see it clearly, but somehow, the valley was dark and filled with grotesque shadows. It was as if the light of the sun simply could not penetrate the gloom of the valley.

Hurrying forward to the perpendicular rock wall, the young prince began to climb. He found that the canyon wall was unusually smooth, with very few irregularities or crevices to use as handholds or footholds. He managed to climb just three or four feet and then could go no further. Disappointed, he slid back to the valley floor.

Josiah began to hike down the valley, carefully inspecting the valley wall and looking for a way out. But he soon found that the entire wall was uniform and unbroken, and as impossible to climb as if it had been fashioned from glass. The valley was not deep—twenty or twenty-five feet at the deepest points—but there was simply no way out. Josiah crossed the little creek that ran through the bottom of the ravine and then inspected the wall on the north side of the valley. But the north wall was just the same—a sheer, smooth barrier that proved impossible to climb.

"There has to be a way out of here!" Josiah exclaimed. "There has to be! And I'm going to find it!" He paused for a drink from the stream, but found that the water was bitter to the taste. Wiping his mouth on his sleeve, he crossed the stream and then resumed his hike down the valley.

Four hours later, defeated and thoroughly frustrated, he dropped to a sitting position on a large rock. *What am I to do? I've hiked at least sixty furlongs, but there simply is no way out of this dark, gloomy valley!* Discouragement swept over him. He suddenly felt extremely helpless, alone, and vulnerable.

He looked around for the dove, but his celestial guide was nowhere to be seen. Thinking that he might find guidance in his book, Josiah opened it and began to read, but the page was difficult to see and the words seemed empty and lifeless. It almost seemed as though the book was no longer meant for him, that King Emmanuel's promises were intended for someone else. Finally, he sighed deeply, closed the book, and replaced it inside his doublet.

Standing to his feet, Josiah once again began to shuffle through the dark Valley of Discouragement. His feet felt as if they were made of lead. He stumbled frequently, often falling and skinning his hands on the rough rocks that littered the valley floor. *No one cares about me,* he told himself mournfully. *I'm alone in this dreary valley and I cannot possibly get out without help from someone else. But no one except Woebegone even knows that I'm down here, and no one cares.*

He thought about Woebegone's words. *Perhaps I really don't matter to King Emmanuel either,* he thought sadly. *I was just a lowly slave—why would he even want me as part of the royal family? I'm unworthy to be a prince!* He sighed deeply. *And I've failed my King again—here I am in a valley from which there is no escape, and it is certain that I will never reach the Castle of Patience.*

"A petition!" Josiah said aloud. "I must send a petition to King Emmanuel, for I now need his help more than I have ever needed it before!" Reaching into his doublet, he withdrew the book and opened it, taking the PRAYER parchment from within. But as he replaced the book within his bosom, a sudden gust of wind snatched the parchment from his hand and sent it fluttering away like an injured bird. Josiah chased after it, but it eluded him. Stunned, the young prince watched in dismay as the precious parchment disappeared into the gloom and darkness.

His lonely heart cried out in misery as he shuffled along in the eerie darkness of the valley. Numb with discouragement, he continued to walk through the valley, still searching the sheer walls for a way of escape from his rocky prison, but deep in his heart he had already given up hope. Woebegone was right—there would be no escape from the Valley of Discouragement.

Woebegone! He's the one who got me into this. He set a trap for me and it worked. He didn't come along to help me over the Mountains of Difficulty; he came to lead me right into a trap.

The young prince sank to the ground in defeat, too overcome with discouragement to go any further. Moments later the sun suddenly dropped below the hills to the west, plunging the Valley of Discouragement into complete darkness. High on the hillside above the valley that held Josiah prisoner, a coyote howled mournfully.

Almost a fortnight later, a thin, tattered scarecrow of a human figure staggered aimlessly along the Valley of Discouragement. Somewhere in the countless miles of heartless wandering Josiah had lost the pack of the King's provisions and he had been forced to survive by eating the yellow, bitter-tasting fruit that grew profusely on the scrubby bushes scattered throughout the valley.

Hearing the sound of cheerful voices, Josiah looked up expectantly. A whitewashed fence bordered the rim of the canyon at that point; just beyond the fence he could see travelers passing by: some on horses, some riding in carriages and other conveyances, some on foot. Apparently, a well-traveled highway ran parallel to the valley. His heart leaped. Help was at hand!

Josiah ran forward. Cupping his hands to his mouth, he shouted, "Hello up there! Will somebody help me?" To his utter astonishment and bitter disappointment, not a single soul looked in his direction. Apparently the travelers couldn't even hear him.

He tried again, louder this time. "Help me! I'm down here in the Valley of Discouragement and I need your help!" Again, there was no response from the travelers above. Without exception, they continued on their way as if he had never called. Taking a deep breath, he shouted as loud as he could. His plea for help echoed and re-echoed across the darkness of the valley, but not a single traveler paused for even a moment.

Can't they hear me? Josiah cried silently. *Can't they see me down here? Can't they see that I desperately need help? Am I invisible to them? Why can they not hear me? Or is it just that no one cares?*

Finally, a bold idea occurred to Josiah and he picked up a small rock. "I'll get their attention one way or another!" he said grimly. He hurled the rock up over the edge of the canyon.

The missile struck the neck of a passing horse. Frightened, the animal reared up on its hind legs, nearly unseating its rider. After a moment or two of intense activity, the man succeeded in bringing his mount under control. He reined the horse close to the fence and angrily shouted down at Josiah, "You down there! Did you throw that stone?"

"I need your help!" Josiah cried, elated at having obtained the attention of one who could assist him. "I fell into this dreadful valley, and I've been down here for more than a fortnight! Will you help me out?"

"Why did you throw that stone? You hit my horse!"

"I'm sorry about your horse, sire, but I had to do something to get someone's attention! I need your help! I am perishing down here. Will you help me?"

The horseman seemed heedless to Josiah's words and to his obvious predicament. "I warn you, lad, do not throw any more stones!" he scolded sternly. "Someone could get hurt."

"But I need your help, sire," Josiah pleaded. "Can you help me out of this valley?"

The man glanced upward as if to check the position of the sun. "I'm late for an important engagement," he replied. "Someone else will stop to help you. But *do not* throw any more stones!" Clucking to his horse, he rode away without looking back.

Josiah picked up another rock. *If you won't help me, I'll find someone who will,* he thought fiercely. *At least I now know how to get people's attention!* He hurled the rock but hit no one, so he fired another. The third missile struck a man's hat, knocking it from his head.

The man retrieved his hat and then strode over to the railing. "You down there!" he shouted at Josiah. "What ails you, lad?" The man was wearing a long, black frock coat and Josiah surmised that he was a man of the Church.

"I need your help, sire! I have fallen into this lonely Valley of Discouragement, and I cannot get out. Would you be so good as to help me?"

"The King helps those who help themselves," the cleric replied. "Think positive thoughts, lad. There is tremendous power in positive thinking. When His Majesty created man's mind, he endowed man with infinite possibilities. There is simply no limit to the good that can be accomplished by the power of positive thinking. Chin up, lad, and always let your thoughts be positive!" With these words, the man walked away, leaving Josiah staring wordlessly after him.

The next person to stop—after her attention was arrested by a well-aimed stone—was a well-dressed woman riding alone in a carriage. After listening to Josiah's plea for help, she rolled her eyes and then turned and drove away without a word.

The next traveler was a priest. He paused at the railing and looked down into the Valley of Discouragement, noticing the young prince before Josiah even had a chance to signal him with a rock. "Oh, please, sire, help me!" Josiah pleaded, falling to his knees and wringing his hands. "I have fallen into this dark valley and cannot climb out unless someone helps me!"

To Josiah's utter astonishment, the priest simply stepped to the side of the highway away from the valley and passed on without a backward glance.

A monk was the next to stop, but only after Josiah bounced a small pebble off the top of his bald head. When Josiah explained his predicament, the monk responded just as the priest did—he simply crossed to the other side of the road and continued on his journey without a backward glance.

Why does no one help me? Josiah thought woefully. *Can they not see how desperately I need their assistance? Are these people too busy to stop and help a fellow traveler? Or am I unworthy of their time?*

Josiah stooped and picked up several more small rocks. "I'll keep trying," he vowed aloud, "until someone stops and helps me out of this wretched valley!" At that moment he spotted a dignified gentleman smartly riding a well-groomed horse. The rider's eyes were not upon the road; he held a small book on the pommel of his saddle and was actually reading as he rode along. Josiah took careful aim and managed to hit the man on the leg with a pebble.

The rider emitted a yelp of surprise and nearly dropped his book. He reined to a stop in the middle of the highway and looked around, trying to spot the source of the flying pebble.

"Down here, sire!" Josiah called, waving his arms in an effort to get the man's attention. "I need your help, sire!"

The rider peered down into the gloom of the valley and frowned when he saw Josiah. "What seems to be the problem, lad?" Closing his book, he rode closer to the rail.

"This is the Valley of Discouragement, sire, and I have been a prisoner in this dreadful place for more than a fortnight! I need your help!"

"Why do you not climb out, lad?" The man asked the question as if the matter was a simple one, but his tone was not unkind. He smiled in a friendly, encouraging way.

"I have tried and tried to climb out, sire, but the walls are perpendicular and there are no handholds. Can you help me?"

"Indeed I can, lad. I'm always glad to help a fellow traveler."

Josiah's heart leaped. Help had arrived at last!

The horseman turned, reached into his saddlebags, and pulled out two items, which he tossed over the railing into the canyon. "I wish you well, lad," the man called as he rode away with a friendly wave. Josiah sprang forward and picked the items up, discovering to his amazement and dismay that the friendly rider had left him two books. The title of the first was *Twelve Steps to Self-Improvement*; the second was titled *Building a Healthy Self-Image*. Josiah shook his head sadly. "I don't need advice; I need someone to care enough to stop and help me out of this valley. Why doesn't someone throw me a rope?"

A short while later darkness descended over the countryside as night came to the land of Terrestria. The rising moon was full, but its silver beams could not penetrate the gloom of the Valley of Discouragement. The wind howled mournfully through the valley like a human wailing in distress. Shivering with cold, Josiah crept beneath the overhang of a huge boulder and curled up to go to sleep, confused and alone and despairing of escaping the valley. Once again, his hopes had been raised and then shattered like a clay pot dashed against the rocks.

Josiah spent the next day attempting to get help from passersby. Again, he used rocks to get people's attention, but just as before, no one was willing to help. He got a variety of responses from the various travelers: some chided him for throwing rocks; some offered useless advice and then hurried on about their business; one lady told him that the Valley of Discouragement was just a figment of his imagination. One sincere young farmer even threw Josiah a length of rope—six feet to be exact—which, of course, proved to be quite worthless. An elderly couple out for a pleasure ride in a dashing landau advised him to ignore his discouragement and "be strong."

"Why doesn't somebody help me?" Josiah cried at last, disgusted and disheartened by the response of his fellow travelers. "I cannot escape the Valley of Discouragement by myself. I need someone to care, someone to help." Finally, he abandoned the idea of receiving help from one of the travelers. Once again, he began searching the valley in hopes of finding a way out on his own.

For the next several days the dejected young prince continued to walk the valley, still seeking a way out of his lonely prison. He came to a pile of loose boulders and a sudden inspiration hit—perhaps he could pile enough boulders against the wall of the canyon to make a ramp high enough to allow him to escape. The project would take days and days, he realized, but at present there seemed to be no other hope of escape from the valley. He set to work with renewed energy and zeal.

After five days of backbreaking work Josiah abandoned the idea. The boulders simply wouldn't stay in place—when he piled them, they rolled off each other, refusing to be piled high enough for the ramp that he had in mind.

Josiah sank to the ground in defeat. "King Emmanuel, I have failed you again," he wept. "What am I to do? I have tried and tried to escape from the Valley of Discouragement, but it's no use. Every idea that I try ends in failure. The travelers on the highway were ready to offer advice, but no one was willing to take the time to actually help me out of here. What am I to do? I'll never make it to the Castle of Patience!"

"Prince Josiah!" a voice called just then. "Is that you? Whatever are you doing down there in the Valley of Discouragement?"

Chapter Fifteen

"Prince Josiah!"

Josiah looked up in astonishment as his name echoed across the Valley of Discouragement. A familiar figure in a golden tunic and green leggings was standing at the brink of the canyon and waving to him. A lyre hung at the man's side. Josiah rushed forward. "Encouragement!"

The cheerful little minstrel knelt at the canyon's edge and called down, "Prince Josiah, what are you doing in the Valley of Discouragement? The last time I saw you, you were at the Castle of Faith, and you were living a life of victory!"

"I've been down here for almost a month now," Josiah replied glumly. "I have tried and tried, but I cannot get out."

Encouragement seemed puzzled. "But how did you get into the Valley of Discouragement? This is not a place for a prince such as yourself."

"I was tricked," the young prince replied, hanging his head. "I am on a quest for King Emmanuel, and I am engaged in a quest for seven castles. A fellow traveler by the name of Woebegone crossed the Mountains of Difficulty with me, and he continually talked about how little King Emmanuel cared for us and how poorly he had provided for us. His evil words entered my heart and caused me to doubt the goodness of my King. As we came down from the Mountains of Difficulty I strayed from the Path of Righteousness and I found myself sliding into this wretched Valley of Discouragement. I am trapped here, and I cannot climb out."

"Woebegone?" Encouragement repeated. "I know of nobody by that name. Describe this rogue, if you would."

"He was incredibly thin and looked as if he was starving to death," Josiah answered. "His raiment was threadbare and his sandals were ready to fall off his feet. He seemed to know his way through the Mountains of Difficulty and I thought that he would be a help to me, but every time he opened his mouth a discouraging word came out."

A dark look of anger crossed Encouragement's face. "I know the rogue. He is my twin brother!"

"Your brother, sire? Woebegone is your brother?"

"Indeed, that rascal is my brother, but his name is not Woebegone. His real name is Discouragement, and he is an agent for our enemy, Argamor. In fact, Discouragement is Argamor's best agent—when Lust or Greed or Temptation fail in their attempts to defeat a child of King Emmanuel, Argamor sends my brother, for he is his most effective agent. Discouragement often succeeds when Argamor's other agents have failed."

Josiah was amazed. "I cannot believe that you two are brothers."

"Language was our mother and Influence was our father. I chose to serve our rightful King, Emmanuel, with music and encouraging words, but Discouragement joined the revolution and aligned himself with Argamor. His words are always filled with hatred and discouragement."

"But he looks so much younger than you!"

"Discouragement is ancient, yet he can make himself to appear to be any age in order to deceive and discourage. Throughout the history of Terrestria my brother has caused the downfall of many good men."

"His words have caused me to doubt the goodness of King Emmanuel, and now I am a captive in this wretched valley. Oh, Encouragement, this has been such a difficult journey. I have wandered in the Desert of Doubt, spent time in the Forest of Self-Pity, and nearly drowned in the Swamp of Bitterness. I have tried to serve my King, but I have failed so many times."

"His Majesty never promised a life of ease, my prince," Encouragement replied gently. "The Path of Righteousness is sometimes difficult, but it is always the best path."

"But how do I get out of this Valley of Discouragement? Can you find a rope somewhere and pull me out?"

"I cannot pull you out. You have to—"

"You're just like all the others!" Josiah shouted angrily, and his voice echoed across the canyon. "Everyone wants to give me advice, but no one cares enough to help me. Go ahead, Encouragement, give me some advice and then leave me here. That's what everyone else has done!"

"I will stay here until you are safely out of this valley," the minstrel promised quietly. "I will not leave you, but you have to get out yourself."

Josiah felt ashamed at his outburst of anger. "I'm sorry, sire. But how do I get out?"

"When your soul is cast down, you have to renew your hope in King Emmanuel. He must be your confidence. Remember that his promises are true, and they are eternal. Think of his goodness to you, and praise and thank him for it." The cheerful minstrel began to softly strum the strings on his golden lyre and a pleasant melody wafted across the gloom of the valley. "Music will lift your spirits, filling your heart with praise and thanksgiving, and enabling you to escape the Valley of Discouragement."

"That's all, sire? That's all it takes?"

"That's actually quite a lot, my prince," Encouragement said, with a slight smile playing at the corners of his mouth. "A heart filled with praise and gratitude is no little thing, Josiah. And there's one more thing that will help tremendously."

"What is that?" the young prince asked eagerly.

"Bring someone else up from the Valley of Discouragement with you. Help another out of the valley, and in doing so, you help yourself."

"But there is no one else down here with me," Josiah argued. "I am alone down here. That is one of the worst things about this valley."

"Oh, but you are not alone," the minstrel replied. "There are many others down there with you, but in your blindness and self-pity you failed to see them."

"Where, sire?" Josiah challenged. "Where are the others?"

"One is over there, beneath that ledge," Encouragement replied, pointing. "In the darkness beneath that ledge lies a man who desperately needs your help. He has been in the Valley of Discouragement much longer than you have. Why not bring him with you?"

Josiah hesitated. "How can I help him?"

"Be a friend to him, my prince. Remind him of the goodness of King Emmanuel. Encourage him to praise His Majesty with you, and together you can walk out of the Valley of Discouragement." Encouragement strummed louder, and the lyre's melodic sound filled the air. "Go now, Prince Josiah, and help another poor soul from the valley in which you are now imprisoned."

Josiah hesitated.

"Go, my prince, go!" Encouragement urged. "There is no need to remain in this dreadful Valley of Discouragement a moment longer. Claim the promises of your King. Sing his praises and thank him for his goodness to you. Encourage your fellow man who lies suffering under that ledge, and together you can walk out of the Valley of Discouragement, free and happy. Go now, Prince Josiah!"

Josiah hurried across the valley with giant strides of determination. For the first time in weeks, he opened his mouth and sang a song of praise to his King. Suddenly the valley seemed a little brighter.

The young prince knelt before the ledge of rock and peered beneath it. A pitiful sight met his eyes. Curled up under the ledge in a fetal position of despair and hopelessness was an old man. His tunic was tattered and threadbare; his skin was wrinkled and shriveled. Hollow, lifeless eyes stared unseeingly above a bushy white beard. The man's breathing was labored and weak; clearly, he was dying.

Josiah seized the arm of the pathetic creature and shook it gently. "Old man," he called softly, "I'm here to help you."

There was no response.

Josiah shook the man's sleeve a little harder, a little more insistently. "I'm here to help you, old man. We do not have to stay in this dreadful valley! Together we can walk out—we can be free again!" But the old man's eyes were filmy and lifeless and he didn't even seem to hear Josiah's words.

Josiah's heart went out to the old man. Here was a fellow human being who had simply given up hope, a man who had simply lain down and was waiting for death. Josiah took a deep breath. *I'm going to help you out of this dreadful valley if it's the last thing I do,* Josiah vowed silently. *I will not let you perish in the Valley of Discouragement!*

Grasping the inert form by the arms, Josiah dragged him gently from beneath the overhang. The old man stirred and weakly raised his head, seeming to see Josiah for the first time. "Nay, nay!" he protested feebly. "Just let me be, lad." His head fell back to the ground.

"You cannot stay here, sire," the young prince told him, lifting the man's shoulders and cradling his head in his arms. "You're going to die here. This is the Valley of Discouragement, and I will not let you perish here."

"Let me be," the old man insisted. "I will die here."

"You do not have to die," Josiah declared. "We can be free from this dreadful valley!"

The old man's eyes looked deeply into Josiah's. "There is no way out, lad. I have tried and tried. I've explored every inch of this cursed valley and I can tell you this—there is no way to escape. Now please, just let me be."

"Nay!" Josiah insisted. "There is a way out. We can be free. All we have to do is claim the promises of our King and praise him for his goodness to us. We can help each other. We can be free!"

The old man was crying softly, but no tears coursed down the wrinkled cheeks. "It's no use, lad, it is no use. We will die here in the Valley of Discouragement. Our King has forsaken us."

Josiah's heart cried out at the words. "Don't say that, sire," he begged. "Don't say that. King Emmanuel has not forsaken us—that is a lie that Argamor and Discouragement would have us believe. Our King cares for us—his love is eternal and never ending."

"He no longer cares for *me*, lad." The words were barely a whisper. The old man's eyes slowly closed.

"He does care for you, sire! He does! That's why he sent me

to help you. King Emmanuel cares for us both."

The old man's eyes flickered open and he stared hard at Josiah. "King Emmanuel sent you to help *me*?"

Josiah was weeping now. "King Emmanuel allowed me to slip into this dreadful Valley of Discouragement that I might help you out," he said softly. "I just now realized why I am here. I am here to help you. Sire, come with me. Together we can trust and praise our King and leave this dreadful valley behind us forever!"

The old man sadly shook his head. "It is too late for me, lad, too late. Go, and escape this valley by yourself. Kindly leave this old man to die in peace now. Just go."

"Nay, I will not!" Josiah exclaimed. "You're coming with me. You do not have to perish in this dark valley, and I won't let you. You *have* to come with me, sire."

Josiah gently lifted the trembling old man to his feet. Placing one skinny, wrinkled arm around his own neck, he tenderly helped the old man across the valley. "Sing!" he urged. "Sing a song of praise to King Emmanuel!"

The old man's head sagged against his chest, bouncing from side to side with each step that Josiah took. His eyes were closed. Half-dragging, half-carrying him, the young prince moved the lifeless form toward the nearest wall of the valley. Josiah took a deep breath and lifted his voice in song, "I sing the greatness of my King, my Lord Emmanuel." A shaft of golden sunlight suddenly pierced the gloom of the Valley of Discouragement like a beacon of hope and promise; the golden rays lifted Josiah's spirits immediately.

"His power is great and far exceeds what mortal tongue or pen can tell," Josiah sang. The sunlight grew brighter; a rainbow appeared above the valley. "My heart is full; I sing for him, and trust that I may serve him well." The darkness of the valley had been almost completely dispelled, and Josiah could now see a golden path leading up to the upper rim of the valley. Lifting the old man in his arms, he hurried toward it.

"Sire, we can make it," he said softly to the silent form in his arms. "Our King has provided a way out of the Valley of Discouragement. We can be free!"

"Sing, Prince Josiah, sing," Encouragement urged. "It is imperative that you continue to praise King Emmanuel."

Josiah took a step upwards onto the golden path. His strength suddenly failed and he sagged to his knees under the burden of the old man's weight. There was an indescribable pressure against his chest, as if there were an unseen hand determined to keep him from escaping the valley. He struggled to breathe.

"Sing, Prince Josiah, sing!" Encouragement cried. "You will not make it out of the Valley of Discouragement unless you continue to praise Emmanuel!"

"I sing the love of my great King," Josiah sang, at once finding the strength to rise to his feet again. "His lovingkindness ransomed me, but why he did, I cannot tell."

A second voice joined Josiah's just then, and the young prince looked down to realize with joy that the old man was singing. "His love led him to die for me," the wizened old man and the young prince sang together. "I trust that I may serve him well."

The old man stood to his feet. Side by side, continuing to lift their voices in praise to their King, Josiah and the old man walked arm in arm to the top of the golden trail. As they took the next step, they both realized that they were now free of the Valley of Discouragement and they both shouted for joy. Breaking into song once more, they again praised the name of King Emmanuel, and the valley below them rang with the joyful sound of their voices.

Encouragement hurried forward, beaming with happiness. "You are free, Prince Josiah, you are free! The Valley of Discouragement is a thing of the past!" Josiah embraced him.

"I am Benjamin," the old man said, "and I am very grateful for your gracious help, Prince Josiah. I would have perished without your encouragement."

Prince Josiah nodded and smiled modestly. "I am thankful that I was counted worthy to serve my King by helping you."

Just then a tall knight arrayed in glistening armor approached the jubilant group. "This is Lord Longsuffering," Encouragement told Josiah. "He is the steward of the Castle of Patience, which is just a furlong from here."

Lord Longsuffering dropped his left hand to the hilt of his sword as he extended his right hand to Josiah. "I am pleased to make your acquaintance, my prince," he said in a pleasant, manly voice. "We have been awaiting your arrival at the Castle of Patience."

Josiah shook his hand. "And I am more than anxious to visit the castle, sire," he replied. "For a time I had despaired of ever seeing it."

He stepped to the rim of the Valley of Discouragement and looked down into the dismal recesses. "I am so thankful to be free at last of this dreadful valley." Movement in the valley arrested his gaze and he stared into the gloom and shadows. Suddenly he could see that there were a number of forlorn creatures still imprisoned in the darkness below. Human beings like himself, they wandered hopelessly through the desolate valley, desperately seeking a way of escape. Their steps were slow and faltering; despair was written upon their faces. As Josiah watched in compassion, he began to see that there were still others in the valley, sitting here and there with slumped shoulders as though they had given up all hope.

Still others were in the condition that Benjamin had been, curled up and ready to die.

"May I go back into the Valley of Discouragement, my lord?" Josiah asked Lord Longsuffering.

"Why would you desire that, my prince?"

"There are others who are still imprisoned in the valley," Josiah replied, as his eyes welled with tears. "Perhaps I can help them find their way out. Perhaps this is why King Emmanuel allowed me to stumble into the valley—that I might learn to help others."

Lord Longsuffering and Encouragement both seemed pleased by Josiah's request. "Well said, Prince Josiah. Take care that you sing King Emmanuel's praises the entire time so that you do not become ensnared again," Lord Longsuffering urged. "And remember that you cannot bring anyone out unless they are willing to come. They must sing their own song of praise to the King."

"I'll go with you," Benjamin offered, "for we can be an encouragement to each other as we walk into this place of treachery."

Half an hour later, Josiah and Benjamin led eleven others up the golden path to freedom. Thirteen voices were lifted in songs of praise to their King, and the desolate valley rang with the joyous sound.

Chapter Sixteen

Prince Josiah paused in the shade of a huge oak to read the map that Lord Longsuffering had given him. "The Path of Righteousness winds its way right through the Land of Worldliness and the Pitfalls of Worldly Wealth," Lord Longsuffering had told him as he prepared to leave the Castle of Patience on his journey to the Castle of Godliness. "Stay on the path, read your book and heed the voice of the dove, and you will be safe. Whatever you do, beware of the Quicksands of Possessions, for they have ensnared many an unsuspecting traveler."

"I will use caution and I will follow the map," Josiah had promised. "I will listen to the voice of the dove. That is one reason that I ended up in the Valley of Discouragement—I failed to listen for his gentle voice."

Lord Longsuffering had smiled. "Well said. You will do fine, my prince. I wish you safe traveling and a pleasant journey."

Josiah traced the route of the Path of Righteousness on the map with his forefinger. "So these are the Quicksands of Possessions that Lord Longsuffering warned me about," he said aloud, looking at a portion of the map that was marked with danger symbols. "I will avoid the quicksands at all costs!"

Glancing at his Shield of Faith, he felt a thrilling yet humbling sense of accomplishment. A row of four glittering jewels now adorned the shield, magnificent tokens of his visits to the first four castles. The emerald, the sapphire and the ruby had been enhanced by the addition of a large, brilliant cut diamond that glowed with a thousand dazzling points of light as if it had a multi-colored fire deep within its heart. Lord Longsuffering had presented the majestic gem to him just moments before he left the castle.

Rolling the map up, Josiah placed it back within his doublet and resumed his journey to the Castle of Godliness. The morning was sunny and warm, and he soon found himself thirsting for a drink. When the trail crossed a stone bridge he left the roadway and went down to the little stream beneath the bridge to quench his thirst. Kneeling upon the grassy bank of the stream, the young prince dipped up a double handful of the cool water.

"Good day, my lord!" a cheery voice greeted him. "I trust that your journey today is a pleasant one."

Josiah raised his head and looked around. The grassy bank was littered with snowy white apple blossoms which in places were clustered so thickly that they looked like drifts of snow. Seated on a small, upright boulder among the fallen blossoms in the shade of a gnarled apple tree was a slender woman. She was arrayed in a glistening gown of solid black silk, and she wore more jewelry than Josiah had ever seen on one woman. Countless chains of gold were about her neck; long, pendant earrings hung from each ear; and her fingers and thumbs were adorned with sparkling rings. A tiny round table in front of the woman held a large, perfect sphere of the clearest crystal.

"Come hither, my prince," the woman crooned.

"I am on a quest for my King and cannot be delayed," Josiah answered shortly. "Please do not attempt to detain me."

"I wouldn't dream of such a thing, my lord," the woman purred. Her voice was as slick as oiled glass.

"Who are you?" Josiah asked suspiciously.

"My name is Prosperity, and I am the Countess of Covetousness," she answered.

Josiah stepped away from her. "I must be on my way."

She made a small gesture toward the crystal sphere. "But have you ever seen spellavision?"

Josiah took one cautious step closer. "What is it?"

"It's a magnificent device, truly magnificent," the temptress replied, caressing the crystal sphere lovingly. "When you look into the depths of the spellavision, you can see all the lovely possessions that others have and you don't."

"Why would I want to see such a thing?" Josiah asked.

"So you can make plans to get those possessions for yourself, of course," Prosperity replied sweetly. "Wealth does have its rewards, you know— power, prestige, possessions, pleasure."

Josiah shook his head. "I have no desire to look at the spellavision. I am Prince Josiah, of the Castle of Faith, son of King Emmanuel himself. I want for nothing—you can offer me nothing that I need or want. My father the King meets all my needs quite nicely."

"I notice that you are walking instead of riding," the countess countered slyly. "Why does your father let you walk, when a prince should ride, and ride in style?" She gestured toward the spellavision. "Look at what Prince Half-Heart of the Castle of Discontent rides! You don't have anything half as splendid as that!"

In spite of himself, Josiah glanced at the spellavision. The image of a richly dressed young prince had appeared in the crystal sphere, and Josiah saw that he was riding a magnificent white charger. In an instant Josiah's heart was filled with longing for a horse like the magnificent one that he had just seen in the crystal of the spellavision. Prosperity slipped her cold arm around Josiah's shoulders. "Quite a splendid horse, is it not, my prince?" she whispered. "I can help you get one just like it."

Josiah pulled away from her. "I don't need a horse like that," he resisted. "When I need one, my father will provide it. I am happy walking."

The countess laughed in his face. "Don't be a fool, my prince. Look at what else I have to offer."

The spellavision flashed with brilliantly colored images, drawing Josiah's attention to it like a magnet. He saw glittering visions of castles and lands and rich clothing and beautiful women and smartly dressed servants and horses and carriages and—Josiah turned away. "I do not need any of it," he said flatly. "My father can provide anything I need."

"What about others?" Prosperity suggested. Her voice was soft, smooth, and tantalizing. "If I provide you with wealth, you can use it to help others." She placed a slender hand on his arm. "Just down the road is a poor farmer struggling to feed his family. Just think what a blessing you could be to him if you were to leave a small sack of silver on his doorstep. But, of course, you cannot give to others if you don't have it yourself."

Josiah thought it over.

"Allow me to take a mere moment of your time to show you something that will be of great interest to you, especially since you are interested in helping others," Prosperity purred softly, drawing Josiah gently from the pathway. She led him around behind an outcropping of large boulders.

"There, my prince. What do you think? Could you not use that to be a blessing to others?"

Josiah stared in astonishment. He was standing at the edge of a large expanse of light-colored sand. Twenty paces away, rising from the sand like an island in the ocean, was the edge of a small mountain. The mountain glittered with a royal treasure: piles of golden coins, huge sparkling diamonds, rubies and emeralds, jewel-encrusted swords and crowns and scepters, silver cups and chalices.

"The jeweled mountain is mine," Prosperity told Josiah, "but I will allow you to take away as much treasure as you can carry. Keep it for yourself, or use it to help others—I care not. The treasure is yours, my handsome prince."

Josiah stared at the glittering treasure, enchanted by its beauty and grandeur. "There is a king's ransom here!" he exclaimed.

"More than that," Prosperity purred. "No king ever had it this good! Take what you wish, my prince. Keep it or give it away, for it matters not to me."

As Josiah stepped forward to make his way across the sand, a voice warned, "Prince Josiah, beware! Stay back, for this evil temptress is setting a trap for you!" A man in humble peasant's clothing leaped in front of Josiah. "Stay back, my prince," he pleaded. "Beware the Quicksands of Possessions. This is a trap to lure the unsuspecting to their doom."

"Quicksands?" Josiah echoed. "I see no quicksands." He looked the peasant over. "Who are you anyway, sire?"

"My name is Contentment, my prince, and I was sent to warn you of the treachery of covetousness and greed. The glittering gold and jewels that you see upon yonder mountain are mere illusions—this is a trap to lure you from the Path of Righteousness. The treasure that you see before you can bring happiness to no one."

"Liar!" the Countess of Covetousness screeched, glaring hatefully at Contentment. "You despicable, filthy liar!" She turned to Josiah. "He seeks to dissuade you from acquiring the treasure so that he may steal it himself. Pay no heed to the lying thief."

Josiah hesitated, uncertain as to whom to believe. The dove flew down and alighted on the rocks. "Prosperity is lying, my prince. Contentment is telling the truth."

"Prosperity is setting a trap for you," Contentment warned. "Behold!" The peasant picked up a large boulder and heaved it out into the middle of the sand. While Josiah watched in consternation, the boulder quickly sank from sight. "Quicksand," Contentment told Josiah. "This entire area is a treacherous bog of deadly quicksand. Prosperity uses the glittering gold and jewels to lure travelers into the Quicksands of Possessions."

As he spoke, a man and woman dressed in rich attire dashed down the trail, paused for just a moment at the edge of the quicksand, and then leaped toward the jeweled mountain. In an instant they were mired in the quicksand and quickly sank from sight, struggling and screaming. Josiah was aghast. "That could have been me."

"Aye, indeed it could have," Contentment agreed. "Prince Josiah, beware of covetousness, for it is a trap that lures many a traveler into the Quicksands of Possessions. There is nothing wrong with having wealth; there is nothing wrong with owning possessions. But when the desire for wealth and possessions becomes more important to a man or woman than the desire to serve King Emmanuel, that person is in danger. Prosperity is an effective agent for Argamor; she has distracted many travelers from the Path of Righteousness and lured them to their doom, and that is why Argamor sent her to try to keep you from reaching the Castle of Godliness. Read your book—it will tell you that your life consists of far more than just the things which you possess."

Josiah looked around. The glittering mountain had disappeared and Prosperity was nowhere to be seen. "Where is Prosperity?" he asked.

"Prosperity is an evil temptress bent on destroying the lives of His Majesty's servants," Contentment replied. "She distracts travelers with her spellavision, places them under her evil spell, and then lures them into the Quicksands of Possessions. When she saw that she could not lure you into the quicksands, she quickly moved on to tempt another traveler."

"But for you, I would have been lured into her trap," Josiah said fervently. "I thank you." He shuddered as he looked at the Quicksands of Possessions, thinking of what could have happened. "Let me ask you a question, Contentment. Are riches evil? Is it wrong to be prosperous?"

"Nay, my prince," Contentment replied emphatically, "riches are not evil. There are many wealthy men who are also good and virtuous men. Nay, riches are not evil, and there is nothing wrong with being prosperous and wealthy."

"Then why did Prosperity tempt me with riches?"

"Riches and possessions are not evil in themselves, but many times they do distract men from the service of their King. How often a man who seeks to be rich will allow himself to become bedazzled by the enchantments of riches and forget his loyalties to his King! The pursuit of wealth begins to consume his thoughts, his time and his energies. He thinks more about acquiring riches than he does about serving King Emmanuel.

"And then, if he *does* succeed in acquiring wealth, many times he will begin to trust in his wealth more than he trusts in his King, and love his wealth more than he loves his King.

Argamor and the temptress Prosperity are aware of all that, and that's why they use the glitter of wealth and possessions to lure travelers from the Path of Righteousness."

The peasant gestured toward the Path of Righteousness. "Continue on your journey to the Castle of Godliness, my prince. Godliness with contentment will provide you with far greater riches than Prosperity could ever have offered."

Josiah followed Contentment up from the treacherous quicksands and onto the solid ground of the Path of Righteousness. "Argamor will do everything in his power to keep you from reaching the Castle of Godliness," the peasant warned the young prince. "The temptress Prosperity was just the first of his attempts to keep you from reaching the castle. Be on your guard, Prince Josiah, for the next part of your journey will not be an easy one."

"What am I facing, sire?" Josiah asked. "Do you know? Can you tell me?"

"The Path of Righteousness traverses the Vale of the Giants," Contentment told him, with a look of intense concern in his eyes. "The vale is a place of trials and extreme danger, but there is no other way to reach the Castle of Godliness. The giants will oppose you and try to keep you from traveling through the vale, but you can be victorious over every one of them."

"How?" Josiah asked. "Pray tell me, sire."

"Go in the name of King Emmanuel, and make good use of your sword. As servants to Argamor, the giants fear the name of your King, and they fear the power of your sword. Any one of them can easily defeat you if you go in your own power, but you can defeat any and all of them in the name of your King. Stay on the Path of Righteousness, and keep your sword handy at all times."

Josiah sat quietly on the grassy hillside under a brilliant blue sky filled with fleecy clouds, totally absorbed in the reading of his book. Below him stretched the hills and valleys of the region known as the Vale of the Giants, and Josiah knew that he was about to experience some fierce battles. In order to prepare himself for the conflicts that he would face, he had decided to spend extra time reading and studying. He was well aware of the fact that he would be victorious only if he was ready with his sword.

The dove flew down from the branch of a tall maple and alighted on a holly bush. "Stay close to me," Josiah pleaded, "for I will need your help in the Vale of the Giants. I cannot do it without you."

"Fear not, for I would never forsake you," the dove replied. "Listen for my voice, and you will be victorious."

An hour later Josiah stood to his feet. "I am ready," he said simply. "Let us face the giants."

"Keep your sword ready at all times," his celestial guide prompted.

Josiah walked quickly down the hillside and entered the vale. The rolling hills on both sides were covered with scores of huge, round boulders. The Path of Righteousness led right through the center of the vale, and Josiah followed it at a brisk pace. He scanned the area carefully, checking the hillsides and glens as he walked, but saw no giants.

"There are no giants here," he said to the dove in a quiet voice. "Perhaps Contentment was wrong."

"Draw your sword," the dove directed. "The giants are upon you!"

Obeying without questioning, Josiah pulled the book from

his bosom and swung it fiercely, transforming it into the glittering, invincible sword. At that instant, the ground beneath his feet trembled as an earthquake shook the vale, and a fearsome crashing sound thundered between the hills. The boulders on the hillside trembled and tottered as if they were preparing to crash down upon the young prince.

Josiah turned and then gasped in terror. Fully a dozen giants arrayed in battle armor stood facing him, carrying swords as long as farm wagons and spears as tall as oak trees. The Giant of Worry was there, as well as the Giant of Anger and the Giant of Doubt. The Giant of Complacency stood glaring fiercely at Josiah; beside him were his brothers, the Giant of Laziness and the Giant of Ignorance. The Giants of Pride, Impatience and Resentment carried huge clubs over their shoulders, and Josiah could easily guess what they intended to do with those. The Giant of Temptation cradled an enormous battleaxe in his huge hands, the very sight of which caused Josiah to tremble in his boots. Giant Eviltongue and Giant Hategood both held gigantic crossbows, which were loaded and at that very moment pointed at Josiah's heart.

"Stand your ground," the dove said quietly. "These giants intend to kill you to keep you from the Castle of Godliness, but there is no need to worry."

"No need to worry?" Josiah whispered back. "Did you take a look at the size of that battleaxe? One blow could cut a hay wagon in two!"

"Prince Josiah, of the Castle of Faith," the Giant of Temptation roared. The sound of his voice shook the trees on the hillside. "Why are you trespassing in our valley?"

Josiah cringed in fear. "What *am* I doing here?" he asked the dove.

"You are here to defeat some giants," the gentle guide

answered. "Use your mighty sword, Prince Josiah, and charge these enemies of your soul in the name of your King!"

Josiah trembled with fear. "Me? Charge them? Shouldn't I be running for my life?"

"Now, Josiah, now!" the dove urged. "The victory is yours, but only if you act in faith."

Josiah raised the invincible sword. "I come in the power of King Emmanuel," he cried, "and for the honor of his name! Stand aside, every one of you!"

A rumble of laughter greeted his demand. "The tiny prince must think that he's dealing with Littlekins again."

"My sword will teach him a thing or two."

"My sword will chop him into mincemeat!"

"Gentlemen, this arrogant bug has invaded our territory! Let's deal with him as we deal with all who do not swear allegiance to our master, Lord Argamor!" Roaring with rage, the fierce giants descended on the young prince with their colossal swords and spears and clubs and battleaxes. Fear tore at Josiah's heart, but, shouting the name of his King and swinging the sword with all his might, he charged directly at his enormous adversaries. Steel met steel, and the valley shook with the force of the conflict.

Moments later, Josiah stood staring in utter amazement, unable to believe what he was seeing. Three of the evil giants lay dead upon the ground, and the others were fleeing for their lives! The astonished young prince took a quick inventory—he had not a single wound; the fearsome weapons of his colossal adversaries hadn't even touched him. He didn't have as much as a scratch! Shaking his head, Josiah gazed at the hillsides where the giants had fled, but they had vanished without a trace.

"Pass through the vale," the dove told him. "Keep your Shield of Faith at hand."

Looking about the vale for signs of the defeated giants, Josiah walked quickly along the Path of Righteousness. The thrill of victory was sweet.

A rumble like thunder caught his attention and he looked upward. Fear caught in his throat. The hillside above him was alive with motion as scores of the huge boulders rolled down upon him. The giants had dislodged the boulders in an attack from which there could be no escape. Josiah turned to run.

"Prince Josiah," the dove called, "stand your ground."

Josiah hesitated, afraid to stand, but unwilling to disobey the voice of his celestial guide. "Those rocks will crush us!" he cried. "There are scores of them, and they each weigh tons and tons!"

"Stand your ground," the dove repeated. "Use your Shield of Faith to repel the boulders sent upon you by the wicked ones."

"The boulders weigh tons and tons!" Josiah protested. "They will crush me!" A rumble like thunder shook the valley as the huge boulders tumbled toward him. They would be upon him within seconds.

"If faith can move mountains," the dove replied, "it can certainly stop boulders. Use your Shield of Faith, my prince."

Josiah stood his ground. Suddenly the boulders were upon him, crashing down on top of him with a thunderous roar that shook the earth. Josiah held his shield high. As the huge rocks struck his shield, they were deflected into the air where they shattered into tiny fragments and disintegrated like puffs of smoke.

Moments later, the hillsides above him were bare of boulders, and the vale was silent. "Continue on your journey to the Castle of Godliness," the dove said quietly. "The giants are defeated. They will not bother you again today."

Chapter Seventeen

Prince Josiah fingered the fifth jewel in his Shield of Faith, a deep purple amethyst that seemed to glow with the light of the heavens. The journey to the Castle of Godliness had not been an easy one, but, looking at the latest jewel, Josiah decided that it had been worth every step. Only two more castles remained on this quest, the Castle of Brotherly Kindness and the Castle of Charity, and then the young prince would receive his last two jewels and be prepared for service to King Emmanuel.

Lord Pureheart, the steward of the Castle of Godliness, had given him details about the journey to the sixth castle. "This will be the shortest leg of your journey," he had said, as he placed the amethyst into Josiah's shield, "and also the easiest. We are less than sixty furlongs from the Castle of Brotherly Kindness. The Path of Righteousness leads through the City of Wounded Hearts, which is not always a pleasant place to visit, but you can learn much if you will but keep your eyes and your ears and your heart open. The castle lies just beyond the city, not more than six or eight furlongs at most. Farewell, Prince Josiah, and have a pleasant journey."

After less than two hours of travel, Josiah found himself nearing the City of Wounded Hearts. It was a bustling, noisy place. The roadway was filled with travelers: some on horses and donkeys, some riding in carriages and wagons and other conveyances, and many on foot. Well-dressed merchants bringing their goods into the city shouted greetings or insults to each other while peasant farmers worked the fields just outside the city walls. The unpleasant sound of angry children quarreling was audible above the other noises of the busy city.

Josiah passed a tiny shack perched beside the road. A skinny peasant was busily hoeing a tiny plot of ground beside the humble cottage. The man looked as if he was ready to collapse from hunger or fatigue, and he leaned on his hoe for a moment of rest as Josiah approached. Josiah spoke politely to him. "Good morning, sire, and a pleasant day to you!"

The peasant turned and looked directly at Josiah, scowled fiercely, and then went back to his work without speaking.

Well, thought Josiah, *did I say something wrong? He acted as if I had just insulted him. Could he not have taken the time to return my greeting?* He shrugged and walked on.

As Josiah passed through the city gate, a heavyset woman leading a small boy with one hand and clutching a large wooden bucket of water in the other moved to one side to step around another traveler. The woman was scolding the little boy as she hurried along, and her attention was not on where she was going. Josiah stepped back to let her pass but she ran right into him, splashing water all over his boots and leggings.

"Bumbling fool!" she raged, dropping the bucket and raising her hand as if she intended to strike him. "Why do you not watch where you are going?"

"I beg your pardon, my good woman, but it was not—"

"Clumsy ox!" the woman shouted, snatching up her bucket and hitting him squarely in the breastplate with it. "Watch where you are going!" The bucket was still nearly half full, so the irate woman upended it over Josiah's head.

The young prince saw what was coming and managed to leap to one side just in time to avoid most of the water. The woman became angrier still and began to shout threats and insults.

Josiah responded in anger. "You should watch where you are going, woman. You are as big as a cow." He hurried away. *Why did she become angry with me?* he asked himself. *She ran into me, and I'm the one who got wet, yet she acted as if the accident was my fault!*

Remembering what Lord Pureheart had told him, Josiah attempted to follow the street through the bustling city but found that the street made one turn after another. Within minutes, he was hopelessly lost. Hurrying down the busy street, Josiah spotted a huge, bearded merchant selling herbs and spices from a small pushcart, so he approached the man to ask for directions. "Pardon me, sire, but is this the road that leads to the Castle of Brotherly Kindness?"

The merchant stared at him with lifeless eyes. "Are you not intending to purchase my wares, lad?" His voice was gruff and impatient.

"I have no money, sire. I am traveling to the Castle—"

"Then step to one side so that others may see my merchandise!" The merchant rudely shoved Josiah out of the way.

Josiah glanced behind him but saw that no one was approaching the merchant's cart. He tried again. "Is this the road to the Castle of Brotherly Kindness? I seem to have lost my way and I thought—"

"Move out of the way, knave!" the merchant shouted, giving

Josiah another shove. "I must sell my wares today, and you will not interfere with business!"

"But sire, I need your help," Josiah replied. "I just need to know—"

"Can you not see that I am a busy man?" the merchant shouted, growing red in the face and snorting like an angry bull. "I have no time for idle chatter. I need customers, not idle talk."

"If you weren't such a churlish knave, perhaps you'd have more customers!" the young prince snapped. He hurried away. *What is wrong with these people?* he asked himself. *Is everyone in this entire city this ill-tempered? I'm glad that I don't live here.*

The narrow, twisting street grew more and more crowded as Josiah walked uncertainly along. He turned a corner to enter a crowded market place. Making his way through the noisy, shoving throng he spotted a well and hurried toward it. The sun was hot, and a drink of water would be quite refreshing. Several townspeople were waiting ahead of him, so Josiah got in line.

An elderly man had pulled a wooden oxcart close to the well. The cart was loaded with eight large water pots, and the man was using the single bucket from the well to fill them. The windlass creaked and protested as the brimming bucket neared the top of the well, and the elderly owner of the oxcart poured the water into one of the pots, filling it to the brim. Josiah saw that three were now full, with five more to go. He sighed. This was going to take forever!

"Come on, old man," a woman leading two goats complained. "Other people are waiting. Are you going to take all day?"

The man stopped what he was doing and rested the bucket on the stone edge of the well. He glared angrily at the goat woman. "I was here before you, woman," he snapped, "so just wait your turn!"

"Well, don't just stand there," another peasant growled. "Fill your water pots and get your flea-bitten animals out of the way."

The old man made an angry face and dropped the bucket down into the darkness of the well. Six or eight minutes later he had completed his task, and all eight water pots were full. He held the bucket out to the goat woman and as she reached for it, turned and dropped the bucket back into the well. With a sneer of contempt for those who were waiting behind him, he struck his oxen with a switch and the wagon lumbered away.

The goat woman cranked a brimming bucket to the top of the well, swung the bucket over the edge, and placed it on the ground to give her animals a drink. "What do you think you are doing, woman?" a huge man with a large, droopy moustache shouted at her. "Don't let those dirty animals drink from the same bucket that I intend to drink from."

The goat woman looked at him with a mocking sneer on her thin features. "I wouldn't concern myself with the goats, you big buffoon," she taunted him, "for I dare say that they are far cleaner than you."

The small crowd around the well laughed at this, and the big man became angry. His face grew very red and his jaws twitched angrily. He doubled up his fists, and for just an instant, Josiah thought that he was going to actually strike the woman.

The goats both had their heads in the bucket at the same time and were drinking noisily. They finished drinking and lifted their heads simultaneously. The woman raised her chin toward the man in a gesture of defiance, tipped the bucket over with her foot, and led the goats away.

The big man seized the bucket and dropped it into the well. "Next time, woman," he roared, "I will throw both of your goats down the well!"

"You are the one who needs a bath," the woman retorted over her shoulder, "not my goats!"

Prince Josiah stood quietly watching the angry exchanges between the townspeople. *Never before have I seen such a place,* he told himself. *These people get so angry over the simplest little things. It's as if they walk around looking for a reason to say an angry word to someone else, or to do someone else a discourtesy.*

The man had brought the bucket to the top of the well and now he placed it on the well's edge. Dipping both hands into the water, he lifted them to his mouth and drank noisily. He sighed deeply with satisfaction and then took another drink.

Josiah waited impatiently. *I'll die of thirst if these people don't hurry.*

The big man had now finished drinking and he handed the bucket to Josiah. But at that moment another man stepped forward and took the bucket from Josiah's hands. "I'm in a bit of a hurry, governor," he said. "I'll just take a quick drink first, if you don't mind."

"I do mind," Josiah retorted, seizing the bucket with both hands. "Why don't you wait until it is your turn?"

The man jerked the bucket away from him. "I intend to drink before you, knave," he said. "What do you intend to do about it?"

Josiah debated drawing his sword but then thought better of it. "I was waiting before you were," he declared. "Now give me the bucket!" He reached for it, but the man jerked it away again. "I was before you!" Josiah shouted. He turned and looked at the other townspeople for support. "Was I not?"

"You don't even belong here," a young girl replied. "Why don't you get out of line and wait till we've all had a turn?"

Josiah was shocked at her words. "I've been waiting just like the rest of you," he retorted angrily, "and I intend to have a drink from the well!" He turned, grabbed the bucket, catching the man by surprise and successfully recovering possession of the vessel.

At once several townspeople seized Josiah, tore the bucket from his grasp, and pushed him away from the well. "This is our well," they chorused, "and you will wait till we have finished!" The man who had first grabbed the bucket from Josiah now had possession of the vessel again and was lowering it into the well.

Josiah was furious. Drawing his sword, he leaped forward and cut the rope, causing the bucket to fall untethered into the dark recesses of the well.

The townspeople screamed with rage. "Kill him!" a woman cried, and the crowd surged forward with murder in their eyes. Suddenly realizing the folly of what he had done, the young prince turned and ran for his life. "He cut the rope on the bucket!" a voice cried. "Get him!" More townspeople joined in the chase.

Josiah was perplexed. Darting through the crowded marketplace, he ran for his life. Up one street and down another he ran, yet the angry crowd still pursued him. As he turned a corner, he ventured a quick glance behind him. The street was filled with the furious people determined to catch him, and they were now less than thirty paces behind him. The angry townspeople were gaining on him.

He spotted a narrow alley to his left and darted into it. Garbage and refuse littered the alley, but he thought that it might provide a good hiding place. Dodging around the piles of debris as he ran, he spotted a huge pile of moldy straw. The perfect hiding place! He ran toward it.

As he bent down to scramble under the straw, Josiah failed to see a door open suddenly behind him. Strong hands grabbed him and jerked him through the doorway, slamming the door behind him. He found himself in darkness with a muscular hand covering his mouth. "Don't make a sound," a stern voice warned him.

Just then the noise of running feet told him that his pursuers had entered the alley. Josiah stood trembling in the darkness as they rushed past his position and continued on down the alley in their frenzied search for him. The strong hands released him. "They're gone now, lad."

Josiah heard the sound of flint striking steel and then saw the yellow glow of a lantern. As the light flared brighter, the young prince was surprised to see an old man wearing thick spectacles. "Who are you?" he gasped in surprise.

"I am Sir Compassion, steward of the Castle of Brotherly Kindness."

Josiah struggled to catch his breath. "I am Prince Josiah, of the Castle of Faith. I am making my way to the Castle of Brotherly Kindness to learn from you."

The old man nodded. "I know."

"Thank you for rescuing me, sire," Josiah breathed. "Those people would probably have killed me if they had caught me! I've never seen such a city—everyone here is mean and ill-tempered! It seems that they just walk about looking for an opportunity to say an unkind word or do something mean."

Sir Compassion gave him a stern look. "Who are you to judge them, my prince? You responded just as badly as any of them."

"But did you see how they treated me?" Josiah protested. "I am a prince, yet these common peasants treated me like dirt. I don't have to take their abuse—I am a prince."

"Then act like a prince," Sir Compassion said sharply. "You are a son of King Emmanuel, yet you were acting like a commoner."

"They had no right to treat me that way, sire."

The elderly steward sighed. "Prince Josiah, this is the City of Wounded Hearts. Every one of these people that you have seen today is carrying a tremendous burden. Many of them still wear the chains of iniquity—they are slaves to Argamor. Surely you remember the misery and loneliness that brings. It does not excuse their selfish behavior, but it does explain it. And yet you, a child of the King, have responded just like one of them. They treated you unkindly, so you got even by cutting the rope at the well."

Prince Josiah hung his head in shame. The steward's words cut him to the heart.

"How would King Emmanuel have responded to these people?"

Josiah was silent.

"Prince Josiah," Sir Compassion said finally, "I need to take you to see the hearts of these people. When you see their hearts you will see why they treat each other the way they do, and why they were so unkind to you."

"Sire," Josiah protested, "I can't go out there!"

"You have to," the steward insisted. "You must see these people as King Emmanuel would see them."

"But they'll kill me! If you saw what happened at the well then you saw how angry they were with me. Sire, I can't go back!"

"You will be safe. They will not recognize you." Sir Compassion unfolded a long, black cape and fastened it around Josiah's shoulders, concealing his garments and his Breastplate of Righteousness. He then placed a huge yeoman's hat upon Josiah's head, completely covering his Helmet of Salvation. A long, gray beard completed the disguise.

Sir Compassion opened the door and Josiah followed him out into the alley. "These will allow you to see the townspeople as your King sees them," the steward told Josiah, handing him a pair of spectacles. "Put them on. You will now see these peasants in a wholly different light, for you will see their hearts and their burdens."

Josiah put the spectacles on and followed the old man from the alley. As they stepped into the busy street, Josiah stopped in utter amazement. "They're wearing chains! Most of the people are wearing chains, just like the ones I wore before King Emmanuel set me free!"

Sir Compassion nodded sadly. "They are still in bondage to Argamor. They lead lives of misery and defeat. Surely you remember the horrors of servitude to Argamor. Perhaps now you will begin to understand why the townspeople treated you as they did." He led the way through the jostling crowd. "Follow me. There is more to see."

Moments later Josiah stopped in the street. "Look! There's the woman who splashed water all over me. It was her fault, yet she was angry at me."

"Look at her heart, Prince Josiah. What do you see?"

Josiah was amazed to discover that the spectacles allowed him to see within the hearts of those around him. He looked at the woman who had been so unkind to him. "Why, sire, her heart is filled with sorrow! Deep sorrow. And she carries a huge burden upon her back."

"Aye," Sir Compassion replied softly. "Her husband was a woodcutter. Just last week he was killed when a tree fell on him. Now she is alone with a little boy to provide for, and she does not know how she will do it. These days her heart is filled with grief and longing for her husband, and with fear of the future. She cries herself to sleep each night. Prince Josiah, can you now find it in your heart to forgive her?"

Josiah's eyes were filled with tears. "Sire, I didn't know," he wept. "I simply didn't know the heavy burdens that this woman was bearing. If only I had known, I would never have become angry with her."

"Her grief does not excuse her unkindness toward you, my prince, but now that you can see her heart I think you will understand."

Josiah nodded silently.

"Come along. There is more to see."

"Behold!" Josiah said a moment later. "There's the merchant who wouldn't take even a moment to answer a simple question. Why was he so unkind to me?"

"Look at his heart, my prince. Tell me what you see."

Josiah put the spectacles on and studied the huge man. "His heart is filled with fear!" he replied in surprise. "Sire, why would a big man like him be afraid of anything?"

"The merchant is going blind," Sir Compassion explained. "He lives in a dark world which is growing darker every day. Would you not agree that the merchant has a reason for fear?"

"He also wears a chain," Josiah observed. "I did not see that when I was talking to him."

"We cannot usually see one another's chains, Prince Josiah. These spectacles allow you to see others as King Emmanuel sees them."

"I did not know," Josiah said, weeping again. "It's no wonder that this poor merchant did not want me to interfere with his sales—he knows that he does not have much time left before he is completely blind." He looked imploringly at his guide. "Can we not help him?"

Sir Compassion pulled a golden sovereign from a purse in his belt. "Give him this."

Josiah approached the merchant's pushcart. "Lad, I have no

time for idle chatter," the man said gruffly.

"I am not here to ask directions, for I now know where I am going," Josiah told him, "but I have come to offer you a gift." He extended the golden coin.

The merchant's eyes widened at the sight of the sovereign. "Lad, I—" He fell to his knees. "Forgive my unkind words, my lord!"

Josiah placed the coin in his hands. "I have already forgiven you, sire," he said softly. "I want you to know that King Emmanuel is willing to remove your chain, if only you will come to him."

A short while later the steward and the prince passed through the city gate. "There is the peasant farmer who had no time to return my greeting," Josiah told Sir Compassion. "Why do you think he was so rude?"

"Look at his heart, my prince. What do you see?"

"His heart is filled with worry and anxiety," Josiah replied, after studying the peasant for a moment or two. "Sire, why is he so troubled?"

"He is a yeoman farmer," the steward explained. "He works one day out of four for the lord of the manor in exchange for the tiny cottage that you see and the tiny plot of ground to work for himself."

"But why is he so worried?" Josiah asked.

"His landlord informed him yesterday that he must now work two days out of four instead of just one. The peasant worries that he will not have the time nor the strength to work his own little field and provide for his family." Sir Compassion put a gentle hand on Josiah's shoulder. "Come, my prince. Let us pass once again through the City of Wounded Hearts and make our way to the Castle of Brotherly Kindness."

Josiah studied the townspeople around him as he followed

Sir Compassion through the noisy city. He was saddened to realize that almost everyone in the city was dragging a heavy chain. All around him he saw men and women, boys and girls whose hearts were made heavy with sorrow, guilt, loneliness and fear. Each and every person that he passed on the street was carrying a burden of one sort or another, some so large that they were staggering under the weight. By the time he and the steward reached the far wall of the City of Wounded Hearts, the young prince was in tears.

He removed the spectacles. "I didn't know, Sir Compassion, I just didn't know. All of these people have burdens!"

"Now you are seeing others as King Emmanuel sees them," the wise old steward said softly. "Had you listened to the voice of the dove, he would have told you to treat these people with kindness, as your King has treated you. But you did not listen to the dove, and you responded with anger and unkindness."

Josiah looked up, noticing for the first time that his feathered guide was perched high above him on the city wall.

"Every day of your life you will be surrounded by people who have burdens," Sir Compassion continued. "Some bear heavier burdens than others, but all have burdens. As a child of King Emmanuel, you must look for ways to ease the burdens of others. Even when you are treated unkindly or unfairly, you must always treat others with the brotherly kindness with which your King would treat them."

Josiah nodded, weeping profusely.

Chapter Eighteen

"But I do not deserve the jewel!" Prince Josiah protested, as Sir Compassion prepared to place the sixth jewel in his shield. "I have not demonstrated brotherly kindness to others! You saw how I treated the peasants in the City of Wounded Hearts." The young prince had spent several days at the Castle of Brotherly Kindness and now was preparing to leave the castle to travel to the Castle of Charity and thus conclude his quest.

Sir Compassion paused with the large fire opal in his hand. The rare jewel was white in color, with a rainbow of iridescent fire that glowed in a variety of brilliant colors each time the gem was turned. "You will treat others much differently now, my prince," he answered, "for you have seen their wounded hearts. There will be times when you will be treated unkindly, and you will be tempted to respond with unkind words and actions of your own. But you are learning to see others as King Emmanuel sees them and to treat them with kindness as he would treat them. The sixth jewel is yours."

The steward knelt and fastened the beautiful opal to Josiah's shield. He stood and embraced the young prince. "The final castle lies ahead, Prince Josiah—the Castle of Charity. Once you reach it and receive your final jewel, the quest is over. I wish you a safe and pleasant journey."

The young prince paused nervously at the edge of a dense forest. There was danger ahead—he could sense it—but he could see no visible cause for alarm. He stepped forward tentatively. There was nothing to indicate that anything was amiss, yet he had that uneasy, spine-tingling feeling that he was in imminent danger. He stopped again, took a deep breath, and looked around.

Releasing his breath between clenched teeth, Josiah entered the darkness of the forest. His chest constricted with fear and his heart pounded madly. He could scarcely breathe. There was still no visible danger and yet he could not get rid of the uneasy feeling in his heart that something was wrong, that his life was in jeopardy. Glancing upward, he caught sight of a flash of white darting among the trees. "I feel fearful," he called to the dove. "Am I in danger?"

"Draw your sword, my prince," the dove replied, "for though you are not in danger yet, you soon will be."

Josiah obeyed. He felt reassured with the glittering sword in his hand. He strode forward with renewed confidence. The rocky trail wound its way down through a sheltered glen where the foliage was thicker and the sunlight could scarcely penetrate. A cold chill crept down Josiah's spine.

"Beware, my prince, the danger is upon you!"

A hideous roar shattered the silence of the forest. Josiah spun around to find himself face to face with an enormous serpent. Pale yellow with black markings, the reptile was huge—his head was more than four feet wide and his scales were larger than Josiah's hand! The giant snake darted toward

Josiah, opening his monstrous mouth as he came, and the young prince saw fearsome fangs nearly two feet long. A long, forked tongue darted in and out like black lightning.

Prince Josiah leaped backward in fear. "What is this monster?" he cried to the dove. "I cannot see much of him, but he must be a hundred feet long!"

"This hideous creature is the Serpent of Selfishness," the dove replied. "Beware that he does not bite you, for his fangs carry a deadly poison that will enter your heart and cause you to lose interest in serving King Emmanuel. Argamor has sent the serpent to stop you from reaching the Castle of Charity."

The serpent struck at that moment, drawing his head fully twenty feet above the earth and then slashing downward like a bolt of lightning. Josiah leaped backward and the deadly fangs missed his legs by less than a foot. Hissing angrily, the murderous reptile struck a second time, again with the speed of lightning. Josiah anticipated the strike and managed to roll behind a huge boulder just in time. His heart trembled when he saw huge coils of pale yellow reptilian flesh gliding noiselessly through the trees as the giant snake moved closer and gathered himself for another strike.

"Stand up to him, my prince!" the dove called. "Use your sword."

The young prince suddenly realized that his hands were empty; he had somehow dropped his sword. He panicked.

The huge head rose high in the air above the rock behind which Josiah was crouching. The enormous tongue darted in and out as the snake scented the air; huge, golden reptilian eyes scanned the forest—the snake was searching for him. The enormous fangs were wet and glistening and dripping a clear liquid. Josiah shuddered, knowing that he was seeing the poison that could take his life.

The glitter of steel in the ferns just beyond the rock caught his attention and he lunged forward, snatching up the precious sword and rolling to his feet in one motion. The Serpent of Selfishness struck at that moment, but the young prince was ready for him. As the gigantic head flashed downward, Josiah swung the mighty sword. Steel penetrated reptilian flesh. Hissing angrily, the giant snake recoiled. The fearsome head disappeared from sight behind a clump of trees.

Spotting a thick coil of pale yellow between two trees, Josiah sprang forward and hacked at it with all his might. A screech like a wildcat's call echoed through the trees and the yellow coil disappeared from sight. Josiah knew that he had inflicted a serious wound. He turned and dashed across the clearing and entered the shelter of the trees.

"Prince Josiah! Beware!"

Josiah turned just as the huge head crashed down through the canopy of branches. Swinging his sword to defend himself, he leaped backward with all his might. The deadly fangs missed him by inches, but the glittering blade of his sword struck home, once again wounding the Serpent of Selfishness. The fearsome head swept upward through the branches and disappeared as quickly as it had come.

Gripping the sword with both hands, Josiah stood ready for another attack. He listened intently, but heard nothing. The forest was silent, as if the birds and the insects of the forest were waiting with bated breath for the outcome of the fierce conflict. Josiah's heart pounded.

He sensed rather than heard movement behind him. Spinning around, he caught sight of the golden, malevolent eyes and the deadly fangs as they drew back into the dense green foliage. The serpent was watching him, watching and waiting for the opportunity for another strike. The Path of

Righteousness ahead was open and inviting, so Josiah turned to dash down it.

"Stand up to the Serpent of Selfishness," the dove called softly. "Slay him with your sword, or he will stalk you all the way to the Castle of Charity. Do not be afraid—the Sword of the Spirit will give you victory."

Trusting the words of the dove, the young prince ventured out into the open. The Serpent of Selfishness struck in fury with a roaring hiss that reverberated through the forest. Two deadly fangs loaded with lethal venom slashed downward. Josiah stood his ground, thrusting upwards with all his might at the giant reptilian head. The mighty blade pierced the snake's mouth between the two fangs, and the Serpent of Selfishness jerked back. He struck again and again, one lightning-quick strike after another in quick succession, but each time Josiah met the deadly strikes with steel. The serpent slowly withdrew, and Josiah's heart leaped. He had won the battle!

The young prince stepped back and lowered the point of his sword to the earth, resting both hands upon the hilt as he caught his breath and watched the colossal reptile retreat. He felt a crushing pressure around his ankle and looked down in horror to discover that the serpent had somehow come from behind and wrapped his tail around Josiah's foot. The serpent's tail whipped through the air, jerking Josiah off his feet and causing him to drop his sword.

Josiah lunged forward with all his strength and managed to grasp the sword with one hand. Rolling over on his side, he hacked at the deadly coil around his ankle. The serpent's grip relaxed and he jerked his foot free. He leaped to his feet again just as the fearsome head came crashing down in yet another strike. Thrusting upward with all his strength, Josiah drove the blade of his mighty sword through the reptile's head.

The Serpent of Selfishness sagged to the ground, defeated and lifeless. Josiah's mighty shout of victory echoed through the forest.

Late that afternoon Prince Josiah hiked wearily down a winding mountain road that meandered around rocky buttes and passed between strange rock formations towering over the roadway. Columns of boulders were stacked upon each other in such unusual arrangements that it looked as if a giant child had placed them there and forgotten them, leaving his toys to weather the eons of time. Josiah could tell from the tracks in the lane that the road was well-traveled, but he had not seen another soul for nearly half an hour. He glanced at the sky. "Less than two hours of daylight left. I hope I make it to the Castle of Charity before nightfall."

A low, moaning noise arrested his attention. He stopped in the roadway. He listened intently for several moments, but the sound was not repeated. "Just the wind passing through the canyon," he said aloud. He started forward.

The moan came to his ears again, and this time there was no mistaking the sound—the cry was that of a human being in terrible pain. He looked around, but saw no one. "Is someone there?" he called softly. "Is someone hurt?"

The idea suddenly occurred to him that the entire situation might be a trap. He glanced around, realizing for the first time just what a lonely, desolate spot he was in. The location was ideal for an ambush—perhaps the wisest course of action would be to leave the area as speedily as possible.

He thought about Sir Compassion's words. "Charity is caring for others," the steward had told him, "even when it involves great expense to oneself." Josiah paused. This might be a place of danger, but perhaps somebody needed his help. He called again. "Is someone hurt?"

"Help me," a weak voice called. "Please, help me!"

Josiah looked around, trying frantically to locate the source of the pitiful cry. He listened intently, but all he heard was the gentle whisper of the wind in the canyon. "Where are you?" he called. "I am here to help you."

"Over here," the unseen supplicant replied. "Please hurry!" The voice was strained and racked with pain, and Josiah forgot all about the possibility of an ambush. Somebody desperately needed his help.

"I am behind this rock," the voice told him. "Please..." The voice trailed off.

Josiah spotted a towering rock formation just above the road. He scrambled around behind it and then gasped in dismay. Lying on the ground was a young man just older than he was. The stranger was dressed in royal clothing very similar to his own, but the garments were torn and bloody. Josiah dropped to his knees beside the other traveler, noting with dismay the bleeding wounds, the pale, death-white skin, and the trembling limbs. The young prince could tell at a glance that the stranger was severely injured.

"What happened?" he gasped.

"I was traveling to the Castle of Charity and I fell among thieves," the injured youth whispered through swollen lips. "They beat me severely, and..." He paused, struggling painfully to breathe, and Josiah waited anxiously. "I—I don't think I'm going to make it," the youth said, with a look of anguish upon his face. "And I am so close to the castle, so close to my... my seventh jewel." He gritted his teeth as a wave of pain passed over him.

"You're going to be all right," Josiah declared, trying to reassure the youth. "I will help you to the Castle of Charity. I am

Prince Josiah, of the Castle of Faith, and I am on a quest to the castle, just as you are. I, too, await my seventh jewel."

"I am Prince Selwyn, of the Castle of Assurance," the injured youth whispered. "I wanted so badly to make it to the Castle of Charity and receive my seventh jewel, but I am afraid that—"

"Don't talk," Josiah admonished him. "Rest and save your strength."

"Do you have water?" Selwyn begged. "I have gone for hours without—"

Josiah nodded and swallowed the huge lump in his throat. "I have water." He uncorked a flask from his pack, and, lifting the other's shoulders, helped him drink.

"That is good," Selwyn sighed, as he lay back down.

"Lie still and rest," Josiah said again. "I will attend to your wounds."

Prince Selwyn's eyes fell shut as Josiah tore a sleeve from his own doublet, wet it with water from the flask, and washed the injured youth's wounds. Tearing more strips of cloth from his own royal clothing, Josiah bandaged the wounds to stop the bleeding. When he had finished, he sat back and watched the young prince. *Prince Selwyn is seriously injured—without adequate care, he will die. I have to get him to the Castle of Charity, but how? I certainly can't carry him!*

Opening his book and plucking the parchment from within its pages, Prince Josiah prepared to send a petition to Emmanuel. He quickly scrawled the following message:

> *"Your Majesty,*
>
> *I have encountered a fellow traveler who is sorely wounded. Somehow I must get him to the Castle of Charity. Please send someone who can help.*
>
> *Your son, Prince Josiah."*

Josiah rolled the parchment tightly, opened his fingers, and watched as the petition disappeared over the looming crest of the mountain. The message had scarcely left his hand when the creaking of a carriage wheel arrested his attention. He sprang to his feet and darted from behind the rock formation. His heart leaped. Coming down the mountain road was a fine brougham coach pulled by four sleek black horses! Josiah leaped into the road and waved both arms to signal the driver. The carriage rolled to a stop less than three paces from him.

"What is the matter, my lord?" the driver, a stout man in blazing red livery, called down.

"A traveler has been hurt!" Josiah replied. "He needs our help. Sire, do you know the way to the Castle of Charity?"

"We are not more than ten or twelve furlongs from it," the coachman responded. "Of course I know the way."

"Will you help us, sire?" Josiah pleaded.

To his immense relief, the driver set the brake and clambered down from the coach. "Show me the one who needs help." Josiah led him behind the formation where Prince Selwyn lay.

"He is in serious need, isn't he?" the coachman remarked, kneeling beside the still, white form. "And he a prince like yourself."

"Sire, will you carry us to the Castle of Charity?" Josiah asked eagerly.

"Certainly, my lord, for a price."

"A price! Aye, but I have no money. And I'm certain that Selwyn has none as well, for he was attacked by robbers. That's how he received his injuries. Please, sire, we have no money, but we need your help!"

"I must be paid," the coachman insisted.

"But we have no money. And my friend will die if he doesn't get help! We must take him to the Castle of Charity!"

"You have something that is just as good as money," the man said slyly.

Josiah looked at him in surprise. "What is that, sire?"

The driver touched the end of his whip to Josiah's Shield of Faith. "The gems, my lord. Give me the diamond and I will carry you and your friend to the Castle of Charity."

"The diamond?" Josiah's heart sank. "I cannot possibly let you have that, sire. I received the diamond at the Castle of Patience. I had to cross the Mountains of Difficulty and travel through the Valley of Discouragement to reach that castle." He shuddered at the memory of the many dark, lonely days in the dreadful Valley of Discouragement.

The coachman laughed. "Aye, but you're a prince. I'm sure that you can easily acquire another jewel to take the place of the diamond."

Josiah shook his head. "You don't understand, sire. I am traveling to the Castle of Charity to receive my seventh jewel and therefore be ready to serve King Emmanuel. I simply cannot arrive at the castle without my fourth jewel. The entire trip will have been in vain."

"I must be paid, my lord."

"But Prince Selwyn is dying! Can you not take him to the castle just to help a fellow human being?"

"Nay, my lord. No diamond, no coach."

"Then take the emerald, or the sapphire. Take the ruby, or even the opal—anything but the diamond." Josiah was desperate. To him, the diamond was the most precious of all the jewels, for he had traversed the Valley of Discouragement to receive it. He could not bring himself to even imagine ever spending another moment in that dreadful place. "Which jewel will you have, sire?" He had resigned himself to losing one of the precious jewels to save the life of Prince Selwyn.

"The diamond, my lord."

"But I cannot give you that."

"It's the diamond or nothing." The man's face was hard and unyielding, and Josiah realized that he meant business. This man simply was not about to negotiate.

"Two jewels, sire," Josiah offered. "Take any two jewels except the diamond."

"Nay, I want the diamond. Nothing else."

Josiah shook his head. "I simply cannot give you that."

"Then there is no reason for me to stay here, is there?" The driver turned and walked toward his coach.

The young prince was in torment. He would give anything to save the life of the young prince who lay dying behind the rock formation, yet he could not bring himself to give up the precious diamond. He could not risk the possibility of another journey through the Valley of Discouragement.

Charity is caring for others, even when it involves great expense to oneself. The words of Sir Compassion rang in his memory like the echo of a brass bell. *I'm on my way to the Castle of Charity, yet I have not yet really learned to care for others as my King would have me do.* He hesitated. *I cannot give this man my diamond! I simply cannot!*

Prince Selwyn groaned. "Prince Josiah," he whispered. His voice fell silent.

Josiah dashed for the roadway. "Wait! Sire, wait! You can have the diamond."

Bitter tears stung Josiah's eyes as he watched the greedy coachman use the blade of a knife to pry the precious diamond from its setting.

Chapter Nineteen

Prince Josiah's heart was heavy as the coach rolled up to the moat of the Castle of Charity. This was the last stop in his quest. He had reached the destination toward which he had struggled for so long, but there was no joy in his heart. Although he had completed the assigned quest, he was missing the most valuable of the jewels, his precious diamond.

There was a bit of consolation in knowing that he had helped a fellow traveler reach his destination safely. Prince Selwyn would live—Josiah was almost sure about that now that he was at the Castle of Charity—and he would receive the last of his seven jewels. For some reason that Josiah had been unable to comprehend, the thieves that had robbed Prince Selwyn had been unable to take his Shield of Faith. Selwyn's seventh jewel would soon shine among the others like the morning star.

Josiah looked at his own Shield of Faith. The hole in the polished surface seemed to him a huge crater, mocking him and reminding him of his failure. "But I helped another," he told himself quietly. "I was able to demonstrate brotherly kindness, as my King would have done. Perhaps it was worth it."

The castle walls loomed above him, dark sentinels against the silver of the twilight sky. "Who approaches the castle?" a sentry challenged. A lantern was lowered at the end of a length of chain, illuminating the approach to the castle.

"Prince Josiah, of the Castle of Faith," the young prince called in reply. "With me is Prince Selwyn of the Castle of Assurance. Selwyn has been grievously injured, so we have hired a coach."

"Advance and be recognized," the unseen sentry called, and Josiah hurried from the coach. A tall knight peered at him from across the moat.

"Prince Selwyn is dying, sire! He needs immediate help!"

"Lower the drawbridge and raise the portcullis," the knight called, and immediately Josiah heard the rattle of chains. Moments later the injured prince was being carried into the castle and the coach had disappeared into the darkness.

"Will he live?" Josiah asked anxiously, as the castle physician leaned over his new friend. Prince Selwyn lay motionless upon a bed in a solar on the first floor of the castle. A cheery fire lighted the circular chamber.

"We have a good supply of the Balm of Gilead, my prince," the physician replied. "Prince Selwyn will be back on his feet by the time the sun rises tomorrow."

A stalwart knight stepped into the solar. "Greetings, Prince Josiah," he said cheerfully. "I am Sir Agape, steward of the castle. We have been awaiting your arrival. Welcome to the Castle of Charity. I understand that you have brought another traveler with you."

Josiah stood to his feet and shook the hand that was offered. "My lord, I am honored to be here."

Sir Agape frowned slightly. "Is something amiss, Prince Josiah? Your countenance tells me that you are deeply troubled."

Josiah struggled to hold back the tears as he displayed his

shield and told the story of the loss of the precious diamond. When he had finished, the castle steward began to laugh.

"The jewels in your shield are simply a reflection of the character that you have acquired in the journey," he explained. "In the hands of that greedy coachman, your diamond will soon become a worthless lump of coal."

"But look at my Shield of Faith," Josiah lamented. "The diamond is still missing. Will I have to repeat my journey to the Castle of Patience to replace it?"

Sir Agape smiled at him. "The diamond was nothing more than a symbol of your journey to the Castle of Patience, my prince. The fact that you were willing to sacrifice it to help another tells me that your quest was successful—you now have true charity in your heart.

"As you were told, the purpose of your quest was that you might learn and grow, that you might become like your Lord, King Emmanuel. This is a great day, Prince Josiah, for today you have shown self-sacrificing charity toward another, just as your King would have done. His Majesty will be pleased, for you have honored him by demonstrating his charity toward another.

"We have plenty of diamonds just as magnificent as yours, and we will replace yours first thing tomorrow morning. On the third day of your stay here at the castle we will have a grand ceremony to present you and Prince Selwyn with your seventh jewels." He smiled suddenly. "Well done, Prince Josiah; you have honored the name of your King."

Just as Sir Agape had promised, the ceremony took place on the third day. It was a grand and glorious occasion, one that Josiah would remember for the rest of his life.

Prince Selwyn and Prince Josiah stood side by side outside the entrance to the great hall, dressed in resplendent royal scarlet robes. Josiah laughed nervously. "This is the moment that we have been waiting for, yet all of a sudden, I almost feel afraid. Do you feel the same thing?"

Selwyn nodded. "It is as if a swarm of bumblebees are flying around in my stomach."

Josiah laughed again. "That is exactly how I feel. I am ready for this, and yet I am apprehensive." He looked happily at his Shield of Faith where a splendid fiery diamond glowed among the other jewels. "The moment has come, Prince Selwyn. Today we receive the seventh jewel."

Sir Agape hurried into the foyer. "Ready, my lords? The ceremony is about to begin!"

A fanfare of trumpets sounded just then, and the doors to the great hall swept open. The immense chamber was crowded with eager spectators, but at the sight of the two young princes, an expectant hush settled over the hall. Prince Josiah and Prince Selwyn stepped forward eagerly and began the triumphant march down the crimson carpet.

A moment of sheer joy swept over Josiah's soul as he realized that he had accomplished his objective and completed his quest. He thrilled in the knowledge that he had honored the name of his great sovereign, King Emmanuel. His heart was full. "My King, I will serve you forever," he whispered.

Glossary

Bailey: the courtyard in a castle.

Barbican: the space or courtyard between the inner and outer walls of a castle.

Battlement: on castle walls, a parapet with openings behind which archers would shelter when defending the castle.

Castle: a fortified building or complex of buildings, used both for defense and as the residence for the lord of the surrounding land.

Coat of arms: an arrangement of heraldic emblems, usually depicted on a shield or standard, indicating ancestry and position.

Crenel: one of the gaps or open spaces between the merlons of a battlement.

Curtain: the protective wall of a castle.

Doublet: a close-fitting garment worn by men.

Ewer: a pitcher with a wide spout

Furlong: a measurement of distance equal to one-eighth of a mile.

Garrison: a group of soldiers stationed in a castle.

Gatehouse: a fortified structure built over the gateway to a castle.

Great hall: the room in a castle where the meals were served and the main events of the day occurred.

Jerkin: a close-fitting jacket or short coat.

Keep: the main tower or building of a castle.

Lance: a thrusting weapon with a long wooden shaft and a sharp metal point.

Longbow: a hand-drawn wooden bow 5 1/2 to 6 feet tall.

Lute: a stringed musical instrument having a long, fretted neck and a hollow, pear-shaped body.

Lyre: a musical instrument consisting of a sound box with two curving arms carrying a cross bar from which strings are stretched to the sound box.

Merlon: the rising part of a crenallated wall or battlement.

Minstrel: a traveling entertainer who sang and recited poetry.

Moat: a deep, wide ditch surrounding a castle, often filled with water.

Portcullis: a heavy wooden grating covered with iron and suspended on chains above the gateway or any doorway of a castle. The portcullis could be lowered quickly to seal off an entrance if the castle was attacked.

Reeve: an appointed official responsible for the security and welfare of a town or region.

Saboton: pointed shoes made of steel to protect the feet of a knight in battle.

Salet: a protective helmet usually made of steel, worn by knights in combat.

Scullion: a kitchen servant who is assigned menial work

Sentry walk: a platform or walkway around the inside top of a castle curtain used by guards, lookouts and archers defending a castle.

Solar: a private sitting room or bedroom designated for royalty or nobility.

Standard: a long, tapering flag or ensign, as of a king or a nation.

Stone: a British unit of weight equal to fourteen pounds.

Tunic: a loose-fitting, long-sleeved garment.

Trencher: a flat piece of bread on which meat or other food was served.

Castle Facts

- The daily affairs of a castle were in the hands of a man called the castle steward. The steward answered to the lord of the castle. In the lord's absence, the steward was in charge of the castle.
- The defense of the castle was the responsibility of the castle constable, or castellan, who had charge of one or two garrisons of knights.
- The castle walls, or curtains, were sometimes as thick as 24 feet!
- A suit of armor usually weighed between 45 and 55 pounds.
- It could take as long as an hour for a knight to get dressed for battle.
- A knight's sword, horse, and armor could cost as much as a peasant's lifetime wages!
- An archer with a longbow could send an arrow over three hundred yards and could fire as many as 15 arrows per minute.
- Some castles kept honeybees. Honey was used to sweeten food and drink.

Becoming a Child of the King

The Chronicles of Terrestria are fiction, of course, but the stories represent truth. The kingdom of Terrestria, as you may have realized, is a picture of planet Earth. The gracious and loving King Emmanuel is a picture of the Lord Jesus Christ. Just as King Emmanuel set Josiah free and adopted him, King Jesus wants to free you from sin and adopt you into His royal family. The Bible tells us how to become the children of God and it's as simple as A-B-C:

Admit that you are a sinner. The Bible tells us: "*For all have sinned, and come short of the glory of God.*" (Romans 3:23) Every one of us has done wrong things and sinned against God. Our sin will keep us from heaven and condemn us to hell. We need to be forgiven.

Believe that Jesus died for you. The Bible says: "*But God commendeth his love toward us, in that, while we were yet sinners, Christ died for us.*" (Romans 5:8) The King of kings, the Lord Jesus Christ, became a man and died for our sins on the cross, shedding his blood for us so that we can be forgiven. Three days later, he arose from the grave.

Call on Jesus to save you. The Bible says: "*For whosoever shall call upon the name of the Lord shall be saved.*" (Romans 10:13) Admit to God that you are a sinner. Believe that Jesus died for you on the cross and then came back to life in three days. Call on Jesus in faith and ask him to save you. He will! And when he saves you from your sin, he adopts you into his wonderful family. You become a child of the King!

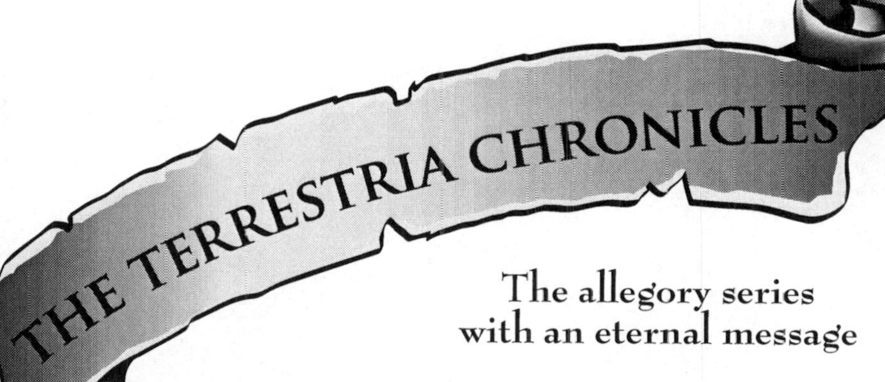

The allegory series
with an eternal message

Looking for the titles you are missing?

Want to share them with your friends?

The Sword, the Ring, and the Parchment

The Quest for Seven Castles

The Search for Everyman

The Crown of Kuros

The Dragon's Egg

The Golden Lamps

The Great War

All volumes available at

WWW.TALESOFCASTLES.COM